jazz guide
new york city

jazz guide
new york city

STEVE DOLLAR

PHOTOGRAPHS
NICHOLAS PRIOR

THE LITTLE BOOKROOM
NEW YORK

First Printing December 2003
Printed in Canada by Transcontinental Printing Co.

Cover image: Jason Moran at Blue Note

Library of Congress Cataloging-in-Publication Data

Dollar, Steve.
Jazz guide New York City / by Steve Dollar;
photographs by Nicholas Prior p. cm.
ISBN 1-892145-19-7
1. Jazz--History and criticism. 2. Musical landmarks--New York
(State)--New York--Guidebooks. 3. New York (State)--New
York--Guidebooks. I. Prior, Nicholas. II. Title.
ML3508.8.N5D65 2003
781.65'09747'1--dc21   2003013853

Published by
The Little Bookroom
1755 Broadway, Fifth floor
New York, NY 10019
212.293.1643 Fax 212.333.5374
editorial@littlebookroom.com
www.littlebookroom.com

Distributed by Publishers Group West;
in the UK by Macmillan Distribution Ltd.

Chapter header captions:
Tribeca & SoHo: Paul Rogers at Knitting Factory; Lower East
Side & East Village: G. Calvin Weston at Tonic; West Village:
Harry Whitaker (piano), Pat O'Leary (bass) at Arturo's; Chelsea:
Stanley Jordan at The Cutting Room; Midtown: Ron Sunshine at
Swing 46; Upper West Side: Billy Drummond at Smoke; Harlem:
Earl May at Lenox Lounge; Brooklyn & Queens: Richie Goods at
Up Over Jazz Cafe; Beyond the Clubs: interior of 55 Bar

TABLE OF CONTENTS

TRIBECA & SOHO

jazz gallery

290 Hudson Street
between Dominick & Spring Streets
☎ 212 242 1063 | www.jazzgallery.org
Ⓜ Spring Street (C·E) Houston Street (1·9)

Given the range of frequently young and unusually adventurous talent that holds forth here, it's easy for anyone who has never been to the Jazz Gallery to mistake it for a serious jazz club. Critics and musicians alike will testify to the curatorial savvy of founder Dale Fitzgerald, who gave up a career in anthropology 24

years ago to plunge headlong into the business end of the New York jazz world, clocking stints at fabled spots like the Village Vanguard and the Tin Palace, and more recently managing trumpeter Roy Hargrove. No doubt, this venue *is* mighty serious. It fosters new work by promising new thinkers, such as pianists Vijay Iyer and Jason Moran, for instance, and boasts Henry Threadgill, one of the music's diehard eclectics, as a resident artist and advisor. Want a sneak preview of some new directions in jazz? Drop by. But don't expect to hear a cash register chime distractingly as the alto saxophonist hits a high note. Because the Jazz Gallery is not a club. It really *is* a gallery. The upstairs space is all polished wood floors, white walls, and folding chairs, and its concept of a "bar" is strictly Episcopal church social: a jug or two of wine and some plastic cups. All the better to focus attention on the music, and the photographic exhibits that often grace the walls. Fitzgerald, a Rhode Island native who introduces performers in the authoritative baritone of a late-night DJ, draws much from his life as a scholar of African music, and uses the venue as a platform for exploring the influences of non-Western cultures on jazz. Along with his partners, he also emphasizes the music's connections to the visual arts, and, as he puts it, "champions the cause of living and growing jazz, rather than creating a jazz orthodoxy based on canonical principles and producing jazz repertory." It helps that the gallery is non-profit (and even chartered by the state of New York as a museum), and can function as a conduit for artists seeking grants and commissions for new work. Musicians get in free, which makes it a good spot for savvy fans to strike up an impromptu conversation with well-known performers who might have happened by to catch a buddy's set.

Beyond its musical ambitions, the venue also exists within a pocket of New York jazz history. Fitzgerald has collected all manner of artifacts that are housed there: the sign from the Tin Palace, an influential Bowery club that enjoyed a resounding run in the late 1970's; the door to Bradley's, the much-lamented oaken piano bar near New York University that was as beloved by musicians as by fans; a piano that belonged to Carmen McRae; an impressive array of jazz poster art. Even its location is a bit mythic. The site, formerly a rehearsal space of Hargrove's bands, sits in what once was known as the city's printing district, a formerly roughneck area not far from the west side docks that was dominated by Italian-owned businesses—at least until the mid-1960's. If you wanted to hear great jazz back then, you would have haunted the Half-Note, a club whose original location is right across the street from the Jazz Gallery. There played Wes Montgomery, Jimmy Rushing, John Coltrane, Lennie Tristano, and Anita O'Day.

Fitzgerald, happy to follow in such giant footsteps, digs up an old clip from *The New Yorker*, an entry in "Goings on About Town" from September 1959, which describes the Half-Note as a "little old Quonset hut converted into a study hall for advanced thinkers. The present set of monitors is under the control of Zoot Sims and Al Cohn. Closed Mondays."

George Colligan and Lonnie Plaxico (bass)

kNiTTiNq fAcTORy

74 Leonard Street
between Broadway & Church Street
☎ 212 219 3006 | www.knittingfactory.com
Ⓜ Canal Street (A·C·E) Broadway (N·R)
Franklin Street (1·9)

Once synonymous with the downtown jazz scene
of the 1990's—in all its free-ranging, cross-pol-
linated glory—this TriBeCa venue's relationship to
the music now is nearly vestigial. The past few years
have seen alternative rock bands and genre-blurring
electronic acts turn the multi-level site into a trend
hub for post-collegiate tastemakers. But the sounds
that built the club's reputation still have a place here.
It's a small one, tucked away like an appendix at
the bottom of four flights of stairs. Dubbed the Old
Office, it's actually the newest of the Knitting Factory's
performance spaces, a renovated sub-basement
named for its former status as a business nook.
It's a cozy, congenially shabby room, with exposed
brick walls, small cafe tables, and a corner booth
that implies something of a 70's steakhouse cocktail
lounge. Performances always feel intimate, almost
like a family gathering, and it's not unusual to spot
avid regulars perched stage-side with a DAT machine
on their table, taping the show (with the artist's
permission, of course). Historically, at least, the Knit
has been bad-mouthed by jazz musicians for all manner of grievances. But the club has fostered long-term
relationships with some of the most consistently novel
and original performers in the city. Bookings at the Old
Office, which was conceived as now-deposed founder
Michael Dorf's answer to the Village Vanguard, sometimes borrow a concept hatched by the Montreal Jazz
Festival: the same artist headlines several consecutive
nights, but leads different lineups. That strategy was
particularly well-suited to a contemporary pool of
New York jazzers, protean types who have too many
ideas for any one group to realize. "It's the right
kind of porridge," says violinist Mat Maneri, who
frequently performs at the Office. "It's not too cold,
and it's not too hot. It's not like you're in a closet
playing for two people in folding chairs. But the room
is small enough so you don't have to overblow. The

Erik Truffaz, with Marcello Giuliani, Marc Erbetta, and Patrick Muller

vibe is that of an old-school, hole-in-the-wall jazz club." Other stalwart spirits—such as saxophonist Tim Berne, pianist Uri Caine, and trumpeter Roy Campbell—have kept the Office buzzing as a legit jazz spot. This, even as second-set patrons are hustled out, drinks in hand, to make way for afterhours DJs.

TRIBECA TUNE-UP

david gage strings

36 Walker Street
near Church Street

☎ 212 274 1322 | www.davidgage.com
Ⓜ Canal Street (A·C·E·N·R·1·9)

Jazz bassists in New York City have but one mecca: David Gage's instrument shop in TriBeCa. It is the beginning and the end of big stringed doghouses and fancy overgrown fiddles, at once a seeming graveyard of scarred old husks and a beauty parlor of burnished, whiskey-colored rhythm machines. The shop, which occupies three floors of an old warehouse space in a once solely industrial stretch of Walker Street, is all dusty countertops and squinty-eyed purpose; its main floor is devoted to repair work, and has been featured as a backdrop for a recent Hewlett-Packard ad. Movie location scouts are likewise in love with the setting, the likes of which is hard to find in the neighborhood these days.

The entrance area also doubles as a gallery. There are perhaps 100 different autographed photos of the shop's clients, and a knowledgeable fan could spend a good hour simply seeking out and identifying individual favorites.

And even if you don't play bass, the workshops hosted here are worth checking out. They usually evolve into much more than a how-to clinic. Contemporary names such as Ron Carter and Dave Holland have entertained, as has Edgar Meyer from the classical side. There is no set schedule for the show-and-tell sessions, which are presented on Mondays or Tuesdays after business hours in a roomy second floor loft space that also is the instrument showroom. Check the website for updates.

ROULETTE

www.roulette.org
[moving to a new location;
address not available at publication date]

Aholdover from the days when SoHo and its environs boasted a thriving gallery and performance loft scene, Roulette may soon be following such predecessors as The Kitchen into new digs. The non-profit organization is in transit, having recently abandoned the TriBeCa loft where it had presented shows since 1980—deep in the heart of DeNiro Country. Overseen by composer and trombonist Jim Staley, Roulette has produced between 50 and 90 concerts a year, securing grants to commission the composers it invites to play. The range is broad, with a strong focus on new jazz and contemporary music works, improvised collaborations, and one-time special events. Under-30 composers are as likely to be heard as such major downtown figures (and board members) as John Zorn or William Parker. Over the years, it's established a small record label (Einstein) and a cable access show (Roulette TV, Fridays at 11pm on the Manhattan Neighborhood Network) that features interviews and taped performances. Like its symbolic casino namesake, there's no telling where Roulette will wind up—Staley anticipates reopening in a permanent location during 2004, and will utilize temporary spaces in the meantime—but, creatively at least, it's a gamble that has paid off handsomely.

s.o.b.'s

204 Varick Street
at West Houston Street
☎ 212 243 4940 | www.sobs.com
Ⓜ Houston Street (1·9)

Going strong since 1982, this is one club where music and dancing are as compatible as rum and Coca-Cola. It's not really a jazz club. The initials are no euphemism, they stand for Sounds of Brazil. But the venue's exceptional taste in all things tropical and subtropical means that fans of what Jelly Roll Morton called "the Spanish tinge" in jazz can indulge fully in various African, Caribbean, and South American sources that have all informed jazz. Dizzy Gillespie collaborated with Mario Bauza, Perez Prado, and Cuban percussionist Chano Pozo in the 1940's. Stan Getz got together with João Gilberto in

the 1960's to coax a craze for gentle samba melodies. More contemporary performers, such as trumpeter Jerry Gonzalez and percussionist Cyro Baptista, keep that fusion of polyrhythms and jazz improvisation at once crisp and seductive.

S.O.B.'s, with its colorful interior and checked tile floors, offers both intimacy—the bandstand is positioned on the long wall, and is buffeted by a table seating area in the rear and an elevated bar area in the front—and elbow room. There's never *any* parking on the dance floor, though the mambo-challenged should drop by Mondays at 7pm for the weekly dance classes that precede La Tropica night. Headliners have included the late Tito Puente, Eddie Palmieri, and the hypnotic Los Munequitos de Matanzas, a catch-'em-when-you-can Cuban percussive outfit whose Santeria rhythms can propel even the least balletic Anglos into hip-twitching ecstasy.

Silvana Magda with Katende Band

LOWER EAST SIDE
& EAST VILLAGE

5c cafe and cultural center

68 Avenue C
at East 5th Street
☎ 212 477 5993 | www.5ccc.com
Ⓜ Second Avenue (F·V)

O nce upon a time in the East Village, the avenues of A, B, C, and D were rough and edgy and riddled with the drug trade. (Well, D still is). But living was cheap, and artists flocked there—decades before the era celebrated in the bohemian rhapsody of *Rent*, itself a symptom of the neighborhood's latter-day gentrification, rather than a defiant expression of paradise lost. Charlie Parker lived on Avenue B opposite Tompkins Square Park in the 1950's. Charles Mingus resided for a while in the mid-1960's on Fifth Street near Avenue A (Sophie's, one of the last great neighborhood pubs, approximates the spot). Slug's, a dive bar on Third Street near Avenue C, was the archetypal Alphabet City jazz dive of the 1960's: You could drop in for a drink, some fried chicken, and hear a wholly catholic range of performers. As swinging as Horace Silver. As astral as Sun Ra. As coruscating as Albert Ayler. If you looked around, most of the musicians weren't even playing. They were just there to hang out. You might have rubbed elbows with John Coltrane or Ornette Coleman. Or, if you were the popular hard-bop trumpeter Lee Morgan ("The Sidewinder"), you would have been shot to death—onstage—by a girlfriend, in 1972.

Despite the influx of trust-fund kids and redevelopment of former squats into high-rent apartments, the East Village is still the best place to bump into workaday musicians and old school poets, happen across a live performance in one of the few remaining community gardens, or find yourself at the Charlie Parker Jazz Festival, staged annually in the park during late August. Start out early enough, and you could also discover the 5c Cafe (also known as 5c Cultural Center), a modest storefront that has been presenting shows, off and on, since 1981. The brainchild of native Philadelphian Bruce Morris, who runs 5c with a partner, Trudy Silver, the space owes its continued existence to its founder's capacity for enduring a succession of legal battles—the explication of which, as you might expect, becomes dizzyingly Byzantine. The upshot, however, is that weekend sets must conclude by 9pm, and weeknight events by 7pm Because he came up against a "judge who hates jazz," Morris can only offer unamplified performances

Andrew Bemkey

on piano, strings, and voice. What's serendipitous is that the reconditioned baby grand Morris has on hand sounds sweeter than most do at the fancy places. And since the room has the feel of a music den, with classic jazz LP jackets prominently displayed, along with photographs and abstract paintings (by 1960's saxophonist Marion Brown), hearing a live performance there is a wonderfully vivid experience. It's a bit like church, or a private listening party, and what shows must legally lack in pyrotechnics is more than made up for by Morris's unabashed advocacy for his cause. He's one of the last of the true believers, the kind of guy who strikes a bare-chested pose on his homepage, hoisting a trumpet in one hand and a bunch of carrots in the other. (The cafe, by the way, serves fresh vegetable juices, as well as caffeinated drinks; alcohol is neither available nor welcome on the premises).

"This is a true community kind of place, the way it used to be 30 years ago," says Morris, who plays DJ Tuesday through Thursday nights, spinning his favorite records for anyone who drops by. Most weekday afternoons around 5pm, there's a solo piano set featuring someone from the neighborhood, young players like Andrew Bemkey or more seasoned ones like Charles Eubanks (a longtime member of saxophonist Dewey Redman's bands). In the spirit of non-profit arts organizations (5C's designation), Silver teaches music classes there, as well. "Oh, man. Those were some times," he continues, clearly sorry to have seen them go, but still holding onto his patch of jazz real estate as if it were a rare postage stamp. "You think about Slug's. It was just this little neighborhood bar, but it was happening!"

ORNETTE COLEMAN OPENS AT THE FIVE SPOT CAFE

Thomas Pynchon dubbed him "McClintic Sphere" for his cameo in the 1962 novel "V.," a jazz outsider making new noises at a joint called the V-Note, where the story's vagabond Whole Sick Crew hangs out. Just three years earlier, the real-life Ornette Coleman, an unknown Fort Worth, Texas native who had arrived via Los Angeles, turned jazz audiences upside down with his debut at the Five Spot on November 18, 1959. Surely Pynchon was in attendance. So was Leonard Bernstein. So was everybody who was anybody in that neighborhood, in those days. The now-legendary club, which then was situated at 4 Cooper Square, became the site for something akin to the riotous debut of Stravinsky's "Rite of Spring." Critics and fellow musicians freaked —and argued. Coleman's quartet, with Charlie Haden on bass, Billy Higgins (or sometimes Ed Blackwell) on drums and Don Cherry on pocket trumpet, took flak for appearing to play "toy" instruments (Coleman's alto saxophone was made of plastic, Cherry's brass was, by definition, child-sized). And worse.

Coleman's use of an untempered scale, and his habit of improvising on the melodic line, rather than the harmony, suggested to many ears that he simply couldn't play. In fact, he was filtering simple folk and blues themes up through Charlie Parker and laying them out in free time, and in the process changing the way in which jazz could be thought about. As Coleman's literary counterpart Sphere (also the middle name of Thelonious Monk, another Five Spot stalwart) philosophizes, he was juxtaposing "crazy and cool in the same molecule." Many disagreed with that hep assessment. As Roy Eldrige told *Esquire* in 1961, "I listened to him all kinds of ways. I listened to him high and I listened to him cold sober. I even played with him. I think he's jiving, baby." But Charles Mingus, another Five Spot regular, offered a more enduring assessment. Coleman was "playing wrong right."

cb's lounge

313 Bowery
at Bleecker Street
☎ 212 677 0455 | www.cbgb.com
Ⓜ Second Avenue (F·V) Bleecker Street (6)

When Charles Mingus coined the expresson "beneath the underdog" to describe the jazz musician's place in society, he probably didn't have this venue in mind. But this basement was, historically, just that. Before Hilly Krystal opened up the now-famous punk club CBGB (and OMFUG) upstairs in the 1970's, the site had been the Palace Bar, watering hole for the Palace Hotel, one of the biggest flophouses on the Bowery. Post-Giuliani, the underdogs have mostly scattered, and New York University is building dorms across the street in what will shortly become a much fancier neighborhood.

But the weekly "freestyle events" staged at the Lounge (downstairs from CB's 313 Gallery) on Wednesday and Sunday nights keep the faith with another Bowery tradition: the no-frills club where musicians can test their new ideas for a crowd that is only there for the music (since, beyond hot pizza and stale draft beer, there's nothing else to savor). Booked by Dee Pop, who in another era drummed for New York rock act the Bush Tetras, the shows offer

Joe Fiedler, John Hebert (bass) Mark Ferber (drums)

good bang-for-buck. A door fee of $8-$10 gets you a set each from four different combos. They vary from working bands to one-off experiments, young bloods from Williamsburg to elder statesmen from Germany and Spanish Harlem, strange collisions of, say, tuba and banjo, to crisp pronouncements regarding the shape of jazz to come.

Roy Campbell

The upstairs 313 Gallery, which offers more of a coffeehouse atmosphere with small art shows and a happier selection of draft beers, occasional picks up some of the downstairs action. Rarely seen drum shaman Milford Graves can pack the space. And downtown crossover acts such as Soul Coughing and Medeski, Martin and Wood enjoyed quality time here a decade ago at the beginning of their careers.

But the scene is really downstairs. "You leave your ego at the door and play for the love of it," says Joe Morris, a highly original guitarist and bassist who has logged more than 20 years of performances in New York, and frequently leads his own groups, or plays in others, at the Lounge. "This is the latest little basement haven. Everybody talks about how great [legendary 1960's] places like Slug's and the Five Spot were, but they were dumps, too. Here, you can let your hair down. It's free of the 'downtown vibe.'"

The long, long rectangular space is a bit odd. If you sit at the bar, the view of the stage is obstructed by the pizza kitchen. Best results come if you go right up front, and sink into one of the beat-up old couches that are the venue's primary decorative scheme. (The lighting over the bar is nifty though, in a George Nelson retro way). Hey, it's a punk rock basement. Waddya want? If the place looks like it was furnished by the Salvation Army, the music can be—in fact—redemptive.

JAZZ HIPSTER HAVEN

downtown music gallery

342 Bowery
between Great Jones & Bond Streets
(East 2nd & East 3rd Streets)
☎ 212 473 0043, 800 622 1387
www.dtmgallery.com
Ⓜ Astor Place (6) Eighth Street (N·R)
Second Avenue (F·V)

Singular in its focus, the Downtown Music Gallery is the kind of record store that could only exist in a novel by Nick Hornby or—the East Village. The typical customers, says owner Bruce Gallanter, "are people with hairy faces." It's the ultimate record collector mecca for those who itch for peculiar niches: the rare 10-CD box-set of futuristic Japanese electro-acoustic improv, the reissued 200-gram vinyl pressing of a long out-of-print record by electric guitar legend Sonny Sharrock, or the latest disc on one of the many artist-owned labels that dominate the lower Manhattan jazz demimonde.

The store, on a transitional block of the Bowery,

belongs to a fondly remembered era before franchises and the Internet revolutionized the music retail business. One reason DMG stays afloat, though, is through its substantial mail-order traffic, and by cornering the market on avant-gardish music—whether jazz, classical, or rock—that can be difficult to find. Gallanter, a tireless advocate for new sounds, publishes a weekly newsletter (also available on the store's website) in which he reviews virtually every fresh release that comes in. He keeps an obsessively completist stock of CDs by downtown cult heroes John Zorn and Bill Laswell, and also maintains a satisfying assortment of used jazz vinyl and classic jazz titles—with a tempting discount CD display which, often as not, will boast a coveted old Wayne Shorter or Don Cherry title.

Artists often sell their product directly to the store, or drop by to check on business, so it's not unlikely for customers to bump into the very performer whose CD they're buying. To make things even easier, Gallanter hosts free concerts every Sunday at 7pm, where the talent can range from the near-novice to the cultishly adored (such as British guitarist Derek Bailey or microtonal saxophonist Joe Maneri). It's not uncommon for the crowd to spill out the door.

Raoul Bjorkenheim and Lukas Ligeti

THE C-NOTE

157 Avenue C
at East 10th Street
☎ 212 677 8142 | www.thecnote.com
Ⓜ First Avenue (L)

Generic East Village pub that it is, the C-Note was among the first new bars to open on Avenue C—back when this block near Tenth Street was a good deal dodgier. Over those years, it's presented jazz as part of a stew that includes alternative rock, blues, and urban hootenannies. Wicked-quirky composer Philip Johnston, whom NPR listeners know penned the theme for "Fresh Air," was a longtime regular with his Transparent Quartet. The current recommendation is to visit Saturdays between 5pm and 7pm to check out Gil Coggins, an old-timer who gigged with Miles Davis, way back when, and has kept his touch.

dETOUR

349 East 13th Street
at Second Avenue
☎ 212 533 6212 | www.jazzatdetour.com
Ⓜ First Avenue (L)

Like a default mechanism, Detour is always there. And there's always a group of aspiring jazz stars playing in the back, every night. Sometimes they grow up to be a drummer like Matt Wilson, or a saxophonist like Rudresh Manhatappa—two widely admired up-and-coming bandleaders with new things to say on their instruments—and they often come back for a visit. Since Detour is a bar first and foremost, and admission is free, it gets a) crowded and b) loud, even on Tuesday nights. So, the fusion-minded acts have an easier time cutting through the noise, and the horn-players have full justification to test their lung capacities. Quiet moments must prevail, however, as former neighbor Norah Jones has namechecked Detour as one of her top Manhattan hangs.

fez

380 Lafayette Street
at Great Jones Street
☎ 212 533 2680 | www.feznyc.com
Ⓜ Broadway-Lafayette (F·V·A·C·E) Bleecker Street (6)

When you hear that Number 4 subway train rumbling down the Lexington Avenue line, and you usually will if you spend any time in this swanky cellar clubroom, those deep bass tremors are a fitting reminder of why Fez is so popular on Thursday nights. For the past decade, the venue downstairs from perpetually trendy Time Cafe has fostered a genuine New York City phenomenon: The weekly performances of the Mingus Big Band.

Mingus, who was ever the most turbulent of jazz composers, also did much to haul the jazz bass out of its supporting role in the rhythm section and into the instrumental spotlight. That rumble might as well be the Big Man himself, never shy about making his presence felt. The late bandleader, who died in 1979 of Lou Gehrig's disease, would no doubt be amused that this ongoing revival of his songbook (the second largest musical archive in the Library of Congress) occurs in a subterranean alcove around the

Mingus Orchestra

corner from the Bowery. It was 1991 when the club's management invited Sue Mingus (the bassist's fourth wife, widow, and posthumous torchbearer) to debut a Mingus ensemble, hoping to add some substance to its bookings. As Sue Mingus remembers, the big band took a slot on the calendar "between a nipple piercing demonstration and an amateur night." These days, the 12-14 piece group—whose members are drawn from a rotating pool of some 200 musicians—anchors the club's schedule (otherwise focused on rising singer-songwriters). Its triumph is threefold: zesty musicianship; a reassertion of big band vibrancy that has long been in decline in the city's jazz clubs; and the remarkable animation of the Mingus canon, which knits together gospel, Afro-Caribbean, rhythm-and-blues, free jazz, and chamber music—usually with the stitches showing.

"He said, 'I'm trying to write the truth of what I am, and the reason it's different is I'm changing all the time,'" says Sue Mingus, an elegant yet formidable presence who maintains a humorously testy relationship with the musicians. The exchange of banter between the bandstand and the center booth from which she holds court is surely part of the Mingus spirit as well. Of course, while Mingus infamously punched in the teeth of his gifted trombonist Jimmy Knepper, the slim and patrician Mrs. Mingus is a good deal more genteel. She simply teases the musician who plays a solo too long or too loud when he comes by for his check. "In the old days, whoever was the leader of the band resented me," she says. "'Who is this woman screeching in the wings?' But then someone said, 'Who pays your checks? She's the leader.' It was a revelation. Now I take it and run with it." The weekly sets rarely skip the Mingus essentials: rousing, gospel-fired numbers like "Better Git Hit in Yo' Soul," and the roaring "Haitian Fight Song" (familiar from Volkswagen and Toyota commercials). But they also explore unknown territory, as Mingus composed much faster than he could get many of his pieces performed. While these Thursday night summits showcase hot soloists taking a break from their own repertoire, they also are popular with performers—such as Elvis Costello—who like to drop in spontaneously. Which, naturally, is how Mingus would have liked it. He was,

Mingus Orchestra

Sue Mingus writes in her memoir *Tonight at Noon*, "the ornery, sometimes violent, often unjust, blustery figure who fired his musicians onstage, hired them back, denounced the audience for inattention, picked fights, mastered his instrument, dominated his music, vented his political beliefs onstage, presented a larger-than-life personality, and created on-the-spot performances for all to see." Mingus rumbles yet.

SUBWAY SOUNDS

It's tough when the critic has a gun," says Tom Bruno. No, the stocky drummer is not engaged in an escalating duel with a scribe gone ballistic. He's joking, sort of, about a key part of his audience. Every week, Bruno sets up his kit somewhere deep in the New York City subway system, joined by musical compatriots who make at least a chunk of their living playing for spare change. The cops who patrol these stations have come to know the clamor of Bruno's sticks as intimately as the rumble of the 4 train as it rolls into Astor Place—one of Bruno's favorite spots.

Not to worry. Bruno, and members of his group Test, have been sanctioned by the city. New York's finest are there to protect them. Unlike, say, the rag-tag doowoppers or amateur breakdancing crews that work the subway cars and station platforms for small coin, these players are part of Music Under New York. The program includes 100-plus acts across a range of musical styles, of which jazz is prominent. Daily performances are scattered across 25 different sites in the system. Test, which also performs in clubs, has been in session for 11 years, its gale-force sound shaped by a natural habitat of squealing brakes and deep subterranean echoes. These musicians play fiercely enough to scare off the subway-dwelling alligators of urban legend, but have won plenty of converts over the years. "When people say they like you, on the subway, that means they really like you," says Sabir Mateen, a tenor saxophonist ubiquitous on the downtown scene, who also gigs with rock bands such as Yo La Tengo. "You can develop a rapport with people down there."

Jazz musicians seem always to have taken to Manhattan's streets. Though income varies, a daily take of $30-$40 up to $100 per person is common. So, for a young, enterprising player, it can provide enough to scrape by while offering a chance to polish technique in a relaxed public forum. Some older artists prefer the pavement to the stage, while others view the subway gig as a useful, but temporary, stop on the way to bigger things. The most famous public musician in New York was Moondog. Blinded at 16 while playing with a dynamite cap, the native

Kansan taught himself to play drums and compose, and moved to New York in 1943. Four years later, he rechristened himself Moondog, and took a spot at the corner of 54th Street and Sixth Avenue, where he held forth for the next 30 years playing a mystery music he called "Snake Time." He made his own instruments—stringed and percussive inventions with names like "oo," "uni," and "samisen"—made records, and achieved a cult following. He favored a Viking helmet and a robe, accessorized by a spear, and wore the long white beard of a Biblical saint—or the old man of the mountain.

Such personal extravagance is rare among rank-and-file subway and street-corner stalwarts. But it does illustrate the freedom such informal stages offer. And, for musicians intrepid enough to hold their ground, it's an acid test of stamina and ingenuity. "Pharoah Sanders told me that he used to try and imitate the train," says Mateen, referring to the saxophonist who rose to attention alongside John Coltrane in the late 1960's, and subsequently became one of jazz's great, latter-day mystics. "I like to think that each sound in the subway is related to a note."

For more information, visit
www.mta.nyc.ny.us/mta/aft/muny.htm#about

joe's pub

425 Lafayette Street
between Astor Place & East 4th Street

☎ 212 539 8777 | www.publictheater.org

Ⓜ Eighth Street (N·R·W) Astor Place (6)

One of the nicest rooms in the city, this lounge and performance space is far spiffier than the work-aday term "pub" connotes. Plush lounge seating, TV studio lighting, and belfry-high ceilings give the two-tiered venue an air of luxury that makes any visit a pleasure—and explains why cocktails are $10 a pop. Named in honor of the late New York Public Theater

Marcia Ball

powerhouse Joe Papp, the Pub formerly served as the non-profit's library, until it was cannily converted into a money-making venture with strong appeal to the music industry. Jazz is a regular attraction on a cal-endar that's otherwise strong on singer-songwriters, major label "tastemaker" showcases, and local artists hip enough for the room. Seating is limited to roughly 100, so most shows sell out quickly (if tickets are even available, as record companies often throw invitation-only events), and standing-room only is a routine op-tion. There's not much argument, however: You won't find a more enjoyable place to hear—and see—live music than this.

knickerbocker
bar & grill

33 University Place
at East 9th Street
☎ 212 228 8490
www.knickerbockerbarandgrill.com
Ⓜ Eighth Street/NYU (N·R·W) Astor Place (6)

The classic, century-old steakhouse near Washington Square offers a vintage, suit-and-tie ambiance in the shadow of New York University's ever-expanding youthplosion. Black leather booths, Hirschfeld sketches framed on the burgundy walls, marble and oak appointments—what's not to love? Besides being the spot sophomore lit scholars are most likely to drag Mom and Dad to on parent's weekend—it's close by, and they take plastic—the Knick has long been a cozy jazz den as well. Live music is featured Thursday through Sunday nights, for a modest $5 cover. The bookings tend toward piano-and-bass duos, with such top shelf names as Cecil McBee, Joanne Brackeen, Hilton Ruiz, Valerie Capers, and John Hicks.

louis

649 East 9th Street
at Avenue C
☎ 212 673 1190
Ⓜ First Avenue (L)

Part of this neighborhood's budding bartopia, Louis is a classic shoebox dressed up in soft hues and exposed brick. And, as it's named in honor of Louis Armstrong, it's got more going on than its wine selection. Live jazz five nights a week with a focus on piano (the bar has two uprights), and John Coltrane on the stereo for later. Record collectors will covet the display of vintage jazz seven-inch singles framed on the walls.

JAZZ AND POETRY

A GATHERING OF TRIBES

285 East 3rd Street
between Avenues C & D
☏ 212 674 3778 | www.tribes.org
Ⓜ Second Ave (F·V)

bowery poetry club

308 Bowery
at Bleecker Street
☏ 212 614 0505 | www.bowerypoetry.org
Ⓜ Second Ave (F·V) Bleecker Street (6)
Eighth Street (N·R)

Langston Hughes and Kenneth Patchen performed with Charles Mingus. Allen Ginsberg's epochal "Howl" evoked "the ghostly clothes of jazz." Contemporary writers who first came to fore in the 1960's, such as Amiri Baraka, Ishmael Reed, and Jayne Cortez, often read in the context of a live jazz performance. Though the two don't always mate naturally, poets and jazz musicians share an affinity for the melodic line, the resonant pause, and the rhythms of breath.

Poet and self-annointed "heckler"—due to his habit of verbally harassing spoken-word newbies at readings—Steve Cannon understands this better than most people. He oversees activity at A Gathering of Tribes which is both the quintessential East Village art space and the name of a journal sufficiently well-regarded to have attracted Wynton Marsalis as a patron. Cannon hosts readings, organizes workshops, presents visual art exhibits, and stages live jazz performances (there's a lush garden in the rear of the classic 19th-century tenement building that's perfect for such occasions). Cannon's a pure character, a blind rabble-rouser whose novel *Groove, Bang and Jive Around* achieved underground buzz status with its raunchy saga of sexcapades in 1960's New Orleans.

You might catch The Heckler some evening at the Bowery Poetry Club. The verb shack of former Nuyorican Poet's Cafe honcho Bob Holman, the club occupies a pleasing, thoroughly renovated street-level site across the street from the once-and-always punk club CBGB. The blonde wood floors are shiny, the ceilings are high, and the staff is friendly: This is not your grandfather's skid row. In fact, if not for the occasionally explicit content of some of the poetry, the BPC could pass for a yuppie fern bar. Besides seemingly constant poetry slams, book parties and one-man shows, the venue boasts weekly zaniness from onetime Andy Warhol superstar Taylor Mead (Fridays, 7pm, $5), and impressive jazz bookings. Reigning downtown jazz capos such as Butch Morris, who leads big band "conductions," and Marc Ribot, a guitarist whose travels have included stints with Elvis Costello and Tom Waits, play here. So, too, has the bassist and bandleader William Parker, and the violinist Billy Bang. Though it's technically a "poetry club," the bar offers much nicer surroundings than most downtown music venues. Maybe it's a sign of the times. Those "ghostly clothes" were overdue for a trip to the dry cleaners.

nublu

62 Avenue C
between East 3rd & East 4th Streets
☎ 212 979 9925 | www.nublu.net
Ⓜ Second Avenue (F·V)

asy to miss, unless you know what to look for: a
single blue light bulb shining over a door. Late
evenings, when this informal wine bar revs up, the
block it occupies is quiet, almost desolate. Next to the
door, a sheet of paper is taped to the wall, with the
day's date and a list of musicians. This is Nublu.

Pass through a second door inscribed with a
hand-written transcript of the Haile Selassie speech
that became the Bob Marley song "War," and you're
in. There's no cover charge, and the setting is typical
of downtown DJ-style hangouts: a pair of turntables
in a back corner, lots of 1960's retro furnishings,
Edith Piaf and Miles Davis album covers as wall art,

a sassy barkeep with a sultry French accent, everyone scruffy-chic and international. At the very back of the room, in what amounts to a second lounge area, a young guitar-based quartet is working through a set of rhythmic near-fusion—kind of David Sanborn gone Williamsburg.

Launched by New York saxophonist Ilhan Ersahin, the club represents an increasingly popular interface between groove-oriented and electronic music and a growing community of jazz musicians and fans in their 20's and early 30's who like to mix beats with their blue notes. Ersahin draws on his connections to various pools of players to create some promising hybrids. (You can hear them on a series of CDs promoted on the club's website). Mingus Big Band saxophonist Seamus Blake is a regular for the midnight show, for instance, with his funk outfit Bloomdaddies, as is trumpeter Eddie Henderson.

RUE b

188 Avenue B
between East 11th & East 12th Streets
☎ 212 358 1700
Ⓜ First Avenue (L)

Only a few years ago, this sort of bistro-with-music would have stuck out like a sore thumb—or a Gold Card—along Avenue B. Too spiffy. Now it's the status quo. The sister restaurant to Radio Perfecto next door, Rue B has swank to burn. An upright Steinway sits in a nook near the restroom, and when musicians play here—as they do every night—patrons have to squeeze by them. If they're sitting close enough, perched on a bar stool, they could join in a duet. Owner Peter DuPre, a onetime actor and entrepreneurial concept guy, collected seating and fixtures from the Stanhope Hotel when the 1930's building was renovated. The walls are lined with Deco-patterned cork or Rat Pack memorabilia. The

John Lang (bass), Roman Ivanoff (piano), John Barnett (sax)

zinc tabletops and bartop convey that industro-diner vibe. The rare XXL movie poster from photographer Bruce Weber's documentary *Broken Noses* (DuPre was a former Weber model) suggests the connoisseur's hand. When a bar is this nice, the music always sucks.

Thankfully, Rue B is an exception. Performers tend to lean towards the singer-songwriter/session dude side of the jazz spectrum. Steely Dan's subversive brainiac, Donald Fagen, has been known to jam when he needs to warm up for a tour (he's a friend of the owners). Other nights, you might catch Cornelius Bumpus, who once played sax with the Doobie Brothers. More frequent is the pianist Joel Forrester, a local favorite who plays every Monday.

TONIC

107 Norfolk Street
between Delancey & Rivington Streets
☎ 212 358 7501 | www.tonicnyc.com
Ⓜ Delancey Street (J·M·Z) Delancey Street (F)

If Paris, as Walter Benjamin once wrote, was the engine room of the 20th century, then Tonic, a bare-bones venue in the heart of the Lower East Side, can lay claim to a similar metaphor. It's very much a salon for all kinds of 21st century music, in permutations that include jazz—and ways that jazz is heard through such prisms as free improvisation, electro-acoustic music (can a Powerbook sing the blues?), DJ culture, klezmer, Asian and European exponents, and good, old-fashioned noise.

Insiders know Tonic as the club that stole the downtown jazz spotlight from the Knitting Factory when it opened in the spring of 1998. That's when club co-founders Melissa Caruso-Scott and John Scott happened on the Tonic site. The 1930's structure had once been headquarters for Kedem, a kosher winemaker, and was being run as a beauty salon (by another couple named Melissa and John, oddly enough). The club opened with a bang: a 40-night series curated by composer and avant-garde ringleader John Zorn, who had recently broken with the Knit, a club that he had been strongly identified with since 1987. Read Biblical significance into the length of the festival, if you will, but Tonic was not quite the land of milk and honey—more like bare concrete floors and no air conditioning. Yet, lines spilled out the door and halfway to Delancey Street, and for many musicians it became a favored venue: Groove merchants Medeski, Martin and Wood; Marc Ribot (guitarist, with Tom Waits and Elvis Costello among others; and bandleader of Los Cubanos Postisos); Zorn's various Masada ensembles; trumpeter Dave Douglas, among many others, including European free-jazz figures who occasionally tour stateside, such as Peter Brotzmann and Derek Bailey. The club's policy of inviting artists to curate month-long programs around a theme often generates fascinating occasions, and its bent for musical arcana reinforces a certain defiant geekiness among the faithful. "It's like being at home," says

Douglas, "and feels like you're playing for family. It's off the beaten path, which is both a big asset and a small drawback. Tonic hasn't tried to become the Disneyland of creative music. But some people who play there aren't going to draw as big an audience as they would in a more central location."

Five years on, Tonic is probably more central than it used to be: the surrounding tenements, which have housed generations of Jewish and, then, Hispanic immigrants, have been steadily converted into renovated coops, while new bars and restaurants arrive daily. Now fully climate-controlled and a little more spruced up, the club has been expanded to accommodate about 250 people. Still, it's nothing fancy. The red curtains that run floor to ceiling behind the stage are the sole concession to décor. The young staff and cultish devotion of the regulars make it easy to think of Tonic as a clubhouse, albeit one without secret handshakes or initiation rituals. The basement space, which is run as a lounge called Subtonic, is more unique. Old kosher wine kegs, which stand tall and

Billy Martin

DJ Logic

wide enough to serve as studio apartments, have been
converted into private seating areas that have the feel of
small wooden cabins. Business is focused on late-night DJ
programs, with an emphasis on electronic soundscapes,
but it's also a good spot to chat with performers before or
after a show. That's when the space becomes a crossroads
between sonic futurism, jazz tradition, and a cyber-savvy
international art culture that's straight out of a William
Gibson novel.

SONNY ROLLINS & THE WILLIAMSBURG BRIDGE

Jazz historians love to disagree, but you won't find many disputing that 1959 was a pivotal year for the music. Miles Davis, Ornette Coleman, and Charles Mingus all recorded classic albums that signified not only artistic vitality, but a form in a heady, transitional stage. The 1960's had begun. But where was Sonny Rollins? The tenor saxophonist had dropped off the scene. Though some of his peers knew where to find him—John Coltrane would practice with him—Rollins had plunged headlong into "retirement." It was anything but, however, as one of jazz's most distinctive soloists was simply "woodshedding." Rollins chose a spot high on the Williamsburg Bridge, not far from his home, to sharpen his chops. He played day and night. Sooner or later, a fan with keen ears was bound to solve the mystery and, sure enough, a writer named Ralph Berton heard Rollins one night, "riding the pulse of a non-existent rhythm section." A subsequent issue of *Metronome* ran the expose, though Berton kept the particulars vague—even changing Rollins' name. But the secret was out. As Rollins told writer Francis Davis, in the liner notes to a reissue of *The Bridge*—the album with which he ended his two-year sabbatical—he chose to retreat after a disappointing gig in Baltimore. "I felt like I wasn't delivering," he said. And began a course of dedicated self-improvement. Jazz lore doesn't get much more romantic. It's irresistible to think of Rollins as the role model for countless, nameless sax players blowing in the moonlight, with the Manhattan skyline in the backdrop. But the reality is: Only one of them will ever be Sonny.

WEST VILLAGE

55 bAR

55 Christopher Street
at Seventh Avenue South
☎ 212 929 9883 | www.55bar.com
Ⓜ Christopher Street/Sheridan Square (1·9)

Considering how much booze moves across its ample bar, which runs the full length of the basement-level space, it's surprising to consider how good and how consistent live music has been at this Greenwich Village staple—for which the term "late night hang" might as well be trademarked.

The bar takes its name from its street address—55 Christopher Street—next door to the former site of the Stonewall Inn, a gay bar where a riot erupted in 1969 after a raid by plainclothes policemen: a watershed moment in the gay liberation movement. Social history is now a plaque. And the neighborhood is quite sedate, save for the occasional mass of drunken collegiates or panhandling street kids. Though the 55 has passed through many hands since opening in 1919—its original owner is said to have won it in a card game on a steamer coming home from World War I—it has sustained its status as a lively music spot since the early 80's. That would approximate the first time electric guitarist Mike Stern plugged in his amp at the former dive bar. Along with guitarist wife Leni Stern, he's been the artist most likely to hold audiences captive here—never missing a Monday

or Wednesday when he isn't on tour. The room fills up quickly, ideal for performers with intense cult followings. The latest shift in management has seen an increased focus on jazz—from fusion and funk-tinged outfits to more left-leaning approaches—with shows every night, and cover charges in the $5-$15 range.

What you can get, on a good night, is an intimate perspective on what many of the city's better young players and bandleaders are thinking about. During a recent week or two, you could have seen bands anchored by in-demand drummers Ben Perowsky and Kenny Wollesen, up-and-coming vocalist Kendra Shank, and hot soloists such as saxophonist Chris Potter and trumpeter Dave Ballou: *musicians'* musicians.

The stage (OK, the floorspace in front of the back wall before you hit the bathrooms) is only part of the story. The 55 also is a place where musicians come to socialize. Cecil Taylor, who became a Picasso of modern-jazz in the 1960's, is supposedly a recluse. (Says so in contemporary music authority Richard Kostelantz's *The Dictionary of the Avant-Gardes*). In which case, the 55 must be the leonine pianist's hermetic lair. "Cecil would be hanging out in the back by the ice machine, for hours, even in daytime, surrounded by the faithful, both wasted and sober," recalls Brian Moran, who served drinks at the 55 for

Marvin Sewell (guitar), Rick Germanson (piano)

Lance D. Bryant

15 years. "He's got a cigarette in one hand, a Brandy Alexander in the other. And he's telling stories. Jazz, Coltrane, Dolphy, dance, Baryshnikov, Martha Graham, history lessons, anecdotes, opinions. Right before he makes a point he always pauses, takes a drag off the ever-present cig: 'And then I said to John ...'"

The 55 is a great place to begin a career or to end one. Norah Jones, Grammy's baby in 2003, got discovered here. Well, in at least one version of her star-is-born creation myth. And not too long before he met his tragic demise 1987, the legendary (and frightfully self-abusive) Jaco Pastorious could be glimpsed in the bar getting dinner. "He grabbed half my sandwich and ate it," Moran says. "And then he said, 'Hi, my name is Jaco. I'm the best goddam bass player in the world.'"

ARTHUR'S TAVERN

57 Grove Street
at Seventh Avenue South
☎ 212 675 6879 | www.arthurstavernnyc.com
Ⓜ Christopher Street (1·9)

Since there's nearly always live music going here, and it's always free, and likewise funky and boisterous, this granddaddy of West Village pubs usually draws one of the youngest crowds allowable by law. This is a nice way of saying that if you're nostalgic for beer-tossed nights on the Quad, Arthur's may be your Santa Claus. The convivial and often patron-stuffed bar has its charms: After more than 60 years in business, it's found a foolproof formula. Part of that is crowd-pleasing music that doesn't overly tax the cerebral cortex. But somehow, pianist Eri Yamamoto manages to engage the ear and still offer something to think about. The Japanese-born player and composer holds down a Thursday-Saturday residency at Arthur's, working the 6:30 to 9pm slot. She's well worth catching, a performer of lyricism and acutely developed tastes who is only the latest promising jazz act to pass under the bar's traditional red awning. The nightspot also claims Charlie Parker as a onetime regular, and also hosted popular trumpeter Roy Hargrove, back when he headlined at cozy corners such as this.

ARTURO'S

106 West Houston Street
at Thompson Street
☎ 212 677 3820
Ⓜ West 4th Street (A·C·E·F·V)

More a Greenwich Village institution than a jazz club, this old-school Italian restaurant nonetheless boasts live music every night of the week. You squeeze by the baby grand piano en route from the bar to the ancillary dining room. Behind the tip jar sits one of the proud, the few, the irascible old guys who hold down those 88's, and have been since the Nixon administration. That's appropriate, since Arturo's represents a warmer, more idiosyncratic phase in the life of its neighborhood, which is bordered by New York University and SoHo. Though its owner and namesake, Arturo ("like Cher," a waiter will joke), has turned over management to his daughter, the walls forever speak his name: They're a personal museum of acquaintance and enthusiasm, crowded with frames of forgotten celebrities and would-be starlets, and a unique collection of this Sunday painter's still-lifes and portraits (Marilyn Monroe is an obvious favorite, and for $150 she can be yours).

The Brick-oven Pizza That Time Forgot is among the city's most satisfying, and the music is, likewise, unfussy, with plenty of cheese dripping off the crust.

James F. Lategano Jr. and Pat O'Leary (bass)

Jimmy Young, who plays Fridays and Saturdays, walked into Arturo's 27 years ago, was asked to sit in on the keys, and never left. Young is an original, a one-man jukebox of jazz standards and forgotten chestnuts whose performances vary according to his mood. Some weekend nights, he's crisp and playful; others, he's a mellow and contemplative as the bar is boisterous. Young and his bassist du jour—the sideman stint at Arturo's has been a rite-of-passage for many young players—play four sets a night. Any of them can resemble something from *American Idol*, as patrons take their turns on the mike: perky Japanese girls, matrons in from Jersey, moonstruck date night couples. You never know. Sometimes, there's a real surprise. Sometimes, you just crave that extra cheese.

blue NOTE

131 West 3rd Street
between Sixth Avenue & MacDougal Street
☎ 212 475 8592 | www.bluenote.net
Ⓜ West 4th Street (A·C·E·F·V)

American vernacular music would not exist without the blue note, which you can explain as something played or sung deeper and darker than routinely called for—flatted, exaggerated, bitten off, made to sting or cry. It's that alchemical element in blues and jazz (and bluegrass and rock) that expresses powerful, wordless feelings. The phrase is at once fundamental and generic, particularly in jazz parlance, where it proliferates: the Blue Note record label is the most recognized name in the fraction of the music industry devoted to jazz, and has the most illustrious back catalog; there's the Duke Ellington song "Ridin' on a Blue Note," first recorded in 1938; and there's the Blue Note. The high-end Greenwich Village jazz club belongs to a chain of venues, including B.B. King's near Times Square—a 1,000-person capacity club that occasionally hosts a star like Sonny Rollins or the

Jason Moran

stray Cuban legend—four Blue Notes in Japan, one in Milan, and a pending expansion into Las Vegas.

Open since 1981, the Blue Note hails from the era when venues such as the Village Gate, the Half Note, the Purple Onion, and Gerde's Folk City were still in business, echoing the vitality of the 1960's. There's a touch of that residual energy still, with the Village Underground, a rock and roots music club, set up directly across Third Avenue. Yet, in many ways, the Blue Note is singular, perched atop the food chain, with its brass-and-mirror décor, $15 cheeseburgers, and a booking policy that tends to lure the kind of names that patrons are willing to pay more to see in such a relatively small venue (though the dining room/stage area is happily spacious for a Village establishment, holding about 200 patrons). This is where pianists such as Chick Corea and Keith Jarrett, who typically fill concert halls, choose to play and record when they want to do a run at a nightclub. This is where 1960's giants Cecil Taylor and Elvin Jones come, on very rare occasions, to reconcile

their individual approaches to piano and percussion. When last they convened for a late-night set at the club, the pair went at it like a couple of old boxers, jabbing as they pleased, as Jones answered Taylor's idiomatic eddies and clusters with the low rumble of tom-toms on the trap set. A dapper fan sat in a chair closest to the stage, eyes rapt at the sight, yet with a stony regard for anyone who might disturb his concentration—which was only fleetingly drawn to his platter of steak. This is where Dizzy Gillespie spent a month celebrating his 75th birthday. This is where Bill Cosby or Stevie Wonder or Kim Cattrall might happen to pop up. If it's a stiffer ticket, well, you get what you pay for, and often enough, you can only get it here. There's a striving for eventfulness to go with the plentiful souvenirs on sale: jazz greats rocking steady a decade past retirement age love to stage birthday concerts here, crowding the stage with special guests and playing way past bedtime. Sometimes, the music moves in ways for which savvy commercial program-ming can't account.

Not every night at the Blue Note is like that, nor could it be, but every so often there's something there when you need it (and still have some headroom left on the credit card).

CORNELIA STREET CAFE

29 Cornelia Street
between Bleecker & West 4th Streets
☎ 212 989 9319 | www.corneliastreetcafe.com
Ⓜ West Fourth Street (A·C·E·F·V)

Like so much about its neighborhood, this restaurant and basement performance space pours on the charm. Doing business since 1977, it's been around just long enough to cultivate an aura: that of the funky but well-vacuumed harbor of quirky creative types, conveniently slotted at the beginning of that picturesque red-brick maze of the West Village. Which is to say, if you leave after consuming too much wine, you can still find your way back to Sixth Avenue.

However, there's no telling where you'll end up once you descend from the upstairs dining room into the basement. On any given evening, the program might be literary (this is where Eve Ensler gave her first public reading of *The Vagina Monologues*, Oliver Sacks is a regular), comic (Francophile pranksters the Cosmic Joke Collective claim this spot as home), or musical. The music is mostly jazz, and mostly worth the time of anyone with an ear for the fresh, the

slightly offbeat, or the mildly exotic. On a weeknight not so long ago, you could have heard the Viennese composer Franz Koglmann, a rare bird in these climes, lead a septet of strings and reeds through a cycle of new pieces that, at times, sounded like a strange chamber dream of Ellington. Critics' faves, like saxophonists Tony Malaby and Bill McHenry, are frequent fliers. All manner of Gallic, Arabic, and Brazilian acts find their way here, as well. Cratin, who often collects the door fee, serves the drinks, adjusts the sound system, and makes sure the piano sounds right, likely never sleeps. But she's effectively cultivated her own salon.

Claustrophobics and guests who have difficulty squeezing into economy class airline seating may find the environs too close for comfort. The 85-person capacity of the basement—a long, narrow shoebox with exposed ceiling pipes offset by a Christmas-y use of color—often feels theoretical. Arrive late for a popular artist, and you'll be making like a sardine back by the tiny bar, making lots of new friends.

Will Holshouser Trio with Ron Horton (trumpet), Dave Phillips (bass)

REMEMBRANCE OF CLUBS PAST

sMall's

Formerly: 183 West 10th Street
at Seventh Avenue South

Few venues are as beloved as this one. Or were. In fact, Small's was every jazz fan's dream. It was genuinely small, a 50-seat club sandwiched into a basement where the audience sat almost on top of the musicians. It was cheap, with a full 10 hours of live music presented daily for $10 (equivalent of a ticket to a 90-minute movie). Sets started early (the first one, at 7:30pm, was free), and didn't finish until sunrise. And as there was no liquor license, patrons were welcome to BYOB. If not, juice and sodas were served gratis. And, finally, many performers who built a following here moved on to bigger and better circumstances. Yet, they still came by for unannounced appearances.

No wonder Small's couldn't stay in business. It was the next best thing to free, a concept that its scholarly constituency (New York University lies close by) could fully appreciate, but that landlords can neither fathom nor respect. When the club closed, after an all-night celebration, on May 31, it had enjoyed a remarkable 10-year run. The monthly rent had tripled from an original $2,650.

"It's too bad you can't make a living playing at Small's," says Joshua Redman, the New York tenor saxophonist who enjoyed one of the biggest breakout careers of the 1990's. "It's really the ideal jazz venue." Though he's among the most public faces in jazz, Redman could be heard at Small's as late as 2001, joining frequent sidemen Brian Blade and Sam Yahel for gigs that led to the formation of a new touring ensemble. "There were these great opportunities to go down there and jam with these guys, and not have to deal with the same kind of attention and pressure I have when I go onstage as a leader."

Mitch Borden, who gave up a nursing career to start Small's, and ate, slept, drank, and fretted over little else but Small's (and its adjacent sister club, The Fat Cat), is possessed of a missionary zeal. Some nights, you would see him playing violin for the lines of people waiting outside the club on West Tenth Street. Small's was more than a business venture for Borden, who mortgaged his house and juggled credit cards to keep the place going. It was a calling, embraced with a generosity and lack of cynicism that's rare in the Big Apple and rarer yet in the club business. He's an enabler, hooked on the idea of gig after gig after gig after gig happening every night in his space. As such, the venue served as workshop and proving ground, but has also fostered what sounds like an oxymoron: a mainstream underground. Small's proved a solid launching pad for promising players of the post-Wynton generation, such as pianist Jason Linder, and bassists Omer Avital and Avishai Cohen, who have both led their own polycultural ensembles to wider recognition. Guitarist Ben Monder, pianist James Hurt, drummer Brian Blade, saxophonists Mark Turner and Greg Tardy—they all found a haven there.

The beaming visage of Louis Armstrong gazed out at the audience from a poster at Small's, whose place in the cosmos of New York nightlife was always something memorable. One incarnation saw the address "become the most infamous spot, Leroy's Hideaway, one of the first gay bars in New York," Borden notes. During the 1960's, it was known as Cafe Wha?, where Jimi Hendrix turned the blues psychedelic en route to the rock'n'roll pantheon. Years from now, Small's will likely lay claim to its own colorful legacy, as talents it nurtured mature into acclaim and the club finds its way into latter-day jazz lore—not unlike such long-gone predecessors as the Village Gate, or the Five Spot Café. "Small's *is* Mitch," Redman says. "You got an audience there that you don't get at other jazz clubs. Younger. Hip—meaning they have fresher ears. People didn't go there just to drink and party. There's an integrity and purity to the feeling. You go into this storefront that you wouldn't even know what it was, and then you make a descent into the subterranean depths of the New York jazz scene. It's got a mythical quality."

FAT CAT

75 Christopher Street
at Seventh Avenue South
☎ 212 675 6056 | www.smallsjazz.com
Ⓜ Christopher Street/Sheridan Square (1·9)

A roomier, more conventional version of the West Village jazz basement, this venue couldn't ask for more unpretentious surroundings. It shares a large, downstairs space with a poolroom. Fortunately, soundproofing and amplification ensures that customers don't confuse the click of a cue-ball with the beat of a snare drum. The Fat Cat, which is split between table seating (closer to the stage) and lounge-like furnishings in the rear, has the convivial ease of an old rathskeller. The room's size, about thrice that of Small's—the much-loved, and now sadly defunct club run by proprietor Mitch Borden (see p. 62)—was meant to accommodate bigger names than its aptly named predecessor, which held sway for a decade just around the corner. Wynton Marsalis has made an appearance—and onetime Small's regulars who have become even slightly bigger names are likely to pay

Kurt Rosenwinkel (guitar) and Chad Taylor (drums)

visits to the bandstand. These include pianist Jason Linder, has moved his weekly big band performances over to the Cat. Though the Fat Cat is a little pricier than Small's—where even the cover charge was small change—it boasts much the same serious attitude about the music. And it may even be possible to make a living playing here.

SWEET RHyTHM

88 Seventh Avenue South
between Bleecker & Grove Streets
☎ 212 255 3626 | www.sweetrhythmny.com
Ⓜ Christopher Street/Sheridan Square (1·9)

Open since September 2002, Sweet Rhythm is a new concept wallpapered over the façade of an older one. The venue occupies the same address as Sweet Basil, a widely appreciated spot that had presented music since the mid-1970's, when the owners of a health-food restaurant popular with local jazzers gradually turned the place into a nightclub. Sweet Basil closed in 2001. But there is continuity. The new incarnation is run by James Browne, who had served as Basil's music director for its last eight years.

Renee Rosnes Quartet: Steve Nelson (vibraphone), Peter Washington (bass)

What's different? The bookings are more international in flavor. "I want the club to represent more the reality of my record collection," says Browne, who spent 17 years as a DJ at Newark jazz station WBGO. "There are enough clubs already doing an excellent job of presenting straight-ahead stuff." The club continues to book plenty of capital "J" jazz, in a relaxed, upscale atmosphere where players feel free to drop by and sit in. Its new direction, though, means a more African tilt.

On any given night, you might get a fast education in the traditional sound of a Senegalese drum choir, or become acquainted with a Nigerian diva. There's even more variety promised by the monthly Rhythm Salon, hosted by trombonist Craig Harris, a multicultural, genre-blurring program that offers a potpourri of vocals, spoken word, and musical performance.

Carrying over from the former club are the high-quality acoustics, which can account for the multiple jazz recordings titled "Live at Sweet Basil." The room slants off the street entrance, one long wall paneled in maple, the other constructed of exposed rustic brick. Browne put in a new lighting design, hanging dozens of Thomas Edison bulbs from the ceiling. Their exposed golden filaments make a subtle complement to the midnight blue decor. Not, jokes Browne, that anything has really changed all that much. "The building dates to 1910 when it was a pharmacy. The bar is where the soda fountain used to be. I like to say that it was originally a pharmacy and it returned to its roots."

village vanguard

178 Seventh Avenue South
at West 11th Street
☎ 212 255 4037 | www.villagevanguard.com
Ⓜ Christopher Street/Sheridan Square (1·9)
14th Street (1·9·2·3)

True seekers of the jazz grail claim the Vanguard as holiest of holies. John Coltrane, as close as the music gets to an official saint, recorded some of his most important work here in the 1960's. So did, on various occasions over the decades, Sonny Rollins, Bill Evans, Joe Henderson, Keith Jarrett, Mel Lewis, Brad Mehldau, Art Pepper, Dexter Gordon, McCoy Tyner, Joe Lovano, Dexter Gordon, Earl Hines, Cannonball Adderly, Dizzy Gillespie, Paul Motian, Tom Harrell, and...the list goes on and on, a litany of geniuses and characters, groundbreakers and traditionalists. At last count, 102 albums or boxed sets have the club's name somewhere in their title or credits. That's the kind of mojo the Vanguard has.

Up and running since 1935, when a law-school dropout named Max Gordon decided he needed a place to hang out, it's the one existing full-time jazz venue in the city that can claim to have shaped musical history. This, even though it wasn't really a jazz club until the 1950's, having previously been a forum for poets and sketch comics, among other entertainments. Before she became a screwball comedy

Dr. Lonnie Smith

queen, Judy Holliday got a leg up there, along with Betty Comden and Adolph Green, in a troupe called the Revuers. Gordon had fancier joints to run, so this humble cellar on Seventh Avenue, shaped roughly like a pizza wedge, sat comfortably on a back burner. Gordon had the smarts to turn the Vanguard into a jazz club about the time network television began absorbing all his regular talent. Smart, because the 1950's and 1960's are now remembered as a prime time for jazz. "He was no expert but he knew what he was doing," says Lorraine Gordon, Max's widow, who presides over the club with a certain imperious authority, shot through with poker-faced wisecracks. "Coltrane. Miles Davis. Dizzy Gillespie. Thelonious Monk. Well, they weren't anybody at the time. They became someone in time, because they were all great and Max knew it." Lorraine Gordon, a Newark, N.J. native, whose first marriage was to Blue Note records founder Alfred Lion, knew who Max Gordon was, but never really had a conversation with him until one day on Fire Island. She began talking about a pianist her husband had recorded. "I booked Thelonious without knowing it. Don't ask me the year. Long ago. He did no business whatsoever and Max bawled me out. Max died in 1989. I continue in his spirit, in his name, in his jollity, in his meanness, in his wonderfulness. I carry the torch," she says, chuckling. "That's the beginning and end of the story."

Well, not quite. The Vanguard's contemporary

profile is strong. Newer talents slip in, such as pianists Uri Caine and Ethan Iverson, if Gordon is enthusiastic enough to embrace them, while regulars return again and again. Wynton Marsalis is a loyal patron, and released a 7-disc boxed set of recordings made on the bandstand. Unshakable keepers of the faith—such as the Heath Brothers, pianist Barry Harris, and the Vanguard Jazz Orchestra, which has played every Monday night for 33 years—bolster the Vanguard's reputation as one place you can hear jazz about which there is no debate: It's definitely jazz. And on rare occasions when there is a shadow of doubt, you might hear a bartender turn critic, slamming the cash register a little bit harder to express displeasure at a particularly gnarly saxophone eruption. "I just tell them never to do it during a bass solo," Gordon says, pausing to note that, hanging above the bar (in the rear corner of the room, stage right) is the euphonium owned by the late trumpeter Jabbo Smith, one of her favorites.

The Vanguard, simply, does not concede. It serves no food (the kitchen serves as both dressing room and business office). It accepts only cash. It will eject or severely tongue-lash patrons unfortunate enough to have left their cell phones on. It only accommodates 120 people per set. "I don't know what people expect when they come here," says Gordon. "It's not Radio City Music Hall. But most of them are entranced by it because it's so pure and original. I do straighten the pictures. And I just put new doors on front. The old ones I'm going to sell on eBay."

Indeed, the club is, itself, something of an arti-fact. The red neon sign that identifies the Vanguard, visible for blocks up and down Seventh Avenue, may not be as iconic as the Empire State Building or the billboards in Times Square, but it signifies something integral to Manhattan and its image. And like the Berlin Wall, it seems, even busted up pieces of the venue are valuable. There's a broken light fixture above the stage that will never be repaired. "The Mingus light," Gordon calls it. "He smashed his bass into it. It's just the hollowed out part of a light. We keep it. It's a shrine. Hey, he ripped off the front doors once!"

Fewer such scenes transpire these days. But while she indulges nostalgia for the days when

Lou Donaldson

jazz seemed as volatile as hip-hop, Gordon has no reservations about her club's—or the music's—future. And certainly none about its present. "If hear one more person tell me jazz is dead, and walk into a jammed room at the Vanguard, I've got to ask: What are they talking about?"

zinc bar

90 West Houston Street
at LaGuardia Place
☎ 212 477-8337 | www.zincbar.com
Ⓜ Broadway-Lafayette Street (F·A·C·E)

Pretty close to the archetype of the "jazz basement," this downstairs room beckons from a
cluster of bars and restaurants along Houston Street,
a block or two from New York University. The interior,
with a cushy red banquette running along one wall
and a bar opposite, feels as seductively candle-lit as
one of those "caves" that dot the Left Bank of Paris,
tight cellars where lovers and musicians convene to
escape the city's bustle. That appeal translates into
true romance—at least, for those who enjoy hearing
performances up close and personal. Even perched on
a barstool near Zinc's entrance, you're almost on top
of the small staging area a few strides away.

The bar features Latin-themed performances on
Thursdays and African sounds on Fridays, with Saturdays and Sundays devoted to Brazilian music. Jazz
fills the rest of the calendar, most notably on Mondays
when guitarist Ron Affif leads the Zinc house band,
which often features the highly respected drummer
Jeff "Tain" Watts. Stick around late enough, or arrive

Gino Sitson

'round midnight, and Zinc becomes an informal jam scene for various local and international stars who are in the habit of dropping by after other gigs—or between tours. Trumpter Roy Hargrove, saxophonist David Sanchez, bassist and vocalist Richard Bona and vocalist Claudia Acuna have all sat in afterhours. It's unpredictable, of course, but one of those value-added attractions that regulars are delighted to take for granted. At $5 admission for all shows (plus a one-drink minimum), it's one of the city's sweetest jazz bargains.

CHELSEA

THE CAJUN

129 Eighth Avenue
at West 16th Street

☎ 212 691 6174 | www.jazzatthecajun.citysearch.com

Ⓜ 14th Street (A·C·E·1·9·2·3)

Want to hear some Dixieland? This is the place to go. The restaurant's music program is all about some early-20th-century New Orleans polyphony, and features musicians who are ardent advocates of the sound and style. It's also the home base for bandleader Vince Giordano, who specializes in recreations of 1920's and 30's jazz. Along with the Nighthawks Orchestra, he revisits classic material from Jelly Roll Morton, Louis Armstrong, and Duke Ellington, among others. The bassist and tuba player is convincing enough that his performances were featured on the soundtrack to *Ghost World*, the film in which Steve Buscemi plays a record collector obsessed with vintage 78 rpm discs.

Giordano, who has led one or another version of his band for 30 years, is such a completist he has to maintain two homes in Flatbush. One for him, and one for his charts. He owns more than 100,000 pieces of sheet music, with some 45,000 arrangements. His performances at the Cajun inspire a committed audience, whose standing reservations mean "they call in only to say that they won't be coming," says guitarist Matt Munisteri, one of the best young musicians making something new out of old-time music, and a sometime guest on the Cajun bandstand. (It's located in the back of the restaurant, but in order to get a seat there you'll have to at least order some gumbo.)

Though some may think such sounds antique –this early jazz, which flourished 80 years ago, steadily attracts a more contemporary audience. The stuff was avant-garde in its day, and played the right way, with a touch of devil-may-care, it still is. "It's got that hot beat," Munisteri says, "that's infectious. No one plays 'hot' these days, it's always 'cool.' But those hot tempos, they're really hard to play!"

THE CUTTING ROOM

19 West 24th Street
between Sixth Avenue & Broadway
☎ 212 691 1900 | www.thecuttingroomnyc.com
Ⓜ 23rd Street (F·V·N·R·W)

Known for its plus-size pours of wine, gentleman's clubroom decor, and rock-star guest lists, this favored stop for entertainment industry insiders also boasts a music room that's one of the city's better-kept secrets. Especially for jazz fans seeking

a change of scenery. While bookings might include anything from a 17-piece all-female accordion orchestra (garbed in Santa Claus caps, no less) to showcase parties for pop singer-songwriters such as Sheryl Crow or Rickie Lee Jones, the venue also hosts a few jazz acts each month. Something like the New York Fusion Ensemble, a 14-piece big band that plays brassy arrangements from the Led Zeppelin songbook, often constitutes the norm; yet, the club might as easily veer towards an evening of heady avant-garde combos. There's no dominant agenda. That appears to please the many musicians who like to drop in to play, onstage or off. The Cutting Room is a favorite with house-band stalwarts from the ranks of *Saturday Night Live*, *Late Night With Conan O'Brien*, and *The Late Show With David Letterman*. The connection makes sense, as co-owner Steve Walter studied composition at the Berklee School of Music in Boston with jazz vibraphonist Gary Burton. Also, his business partner is the popular New York actor Chris Noth (the commitment phobic "Big" from HBO's *Sex and the City*, and a longtime cast member of NBC's *Law and Order*). Seems Noth wanted a place of his own to hang out and hear the music he liked, in a setting that suited his taste, and where his friends would feel comfortable. Hence, the Cutting Room, which opened in 1999 in a cavernous warehouse space in Chelsea that had once housed materials for movie sets.

das neues kabarett at the brecht forum

122 West 27th Street
between Sixth & Seventh Avenues
☎ 212 242 4201 | www.brechtforum.org
Ⓜ 23rd Street (F·V·N·R·W)

Easily among the least-obvious jazz occasions in town, Das Neues Kabarett is the name for the irregularly scheduled live music nights staged at the Brecht Forum, a Marxist study and resource center located 10 floors up inside an anonymous building on a gray industrial block. First-time patrons should definitely consult the website for particulars, though it's not that hard to find. The decidedly unsexy setting, which resembles a library in a community center, should not deter listeners eager to hear new music. Shows here, with admissions in the $10-and-under range, can prove exceptional. They tend to showcase one-of-a-kind players and their acolytes, all focused on a more freely structured approach to performance (open-ended pieces rather than "tunes"). While this bodes self-indulgence, the results frequently are revelatory, as the venue serves as a safe bet for adventurous artists who shun the regular club circuit. The not-for-profit setup means you toss a couple of bucks in a jar for a glass of wine, and earn bohemian brownie points for applauding, say, an impromptu spoken-word piece.

THE KITCHEN

512 West 19th Street
between Tenth & Eleventh Avenues
☎ 212 255 5793 | www.thekitchen.org
Ⓜ 14th Street (A·C·E)

This eminent arts space is devoted to performances of dance, new music, mixed media and theatrical works, with an emphasis on premieres, unveilings, retrospectives, and unique collaborations. Jazz is a vital aspect of this, even as a tangent. A 2003 celebration of the contemporary classical pianist Frederic Rzewski welcomed disparate jazzers Arturo O'Farrill and Matthew Shipp as opening acts. And an ongoing program of commissions finds all manner of New York player-composers—from jazz, improv, and new music scenes—getting the "Kitchen House Blend" treatment. Basically, a crack "house band" featuring a mix of classical and jazz players (including reedist J.D. Parran and trumpeter Ravi Best) learns and performs a trio of new pieces written for the occasion. The shows open a fascinating window on the creative process, while also offering fresh perspectives on the work of musicians who may not often be interpreted in such a way. Plus, a post-show Q&A that usually leads to a few further insights. The venue, pretty much your industrial black box with bleachers and fancy lighting design, is smack in the middle of the meat-packing district, and not far from the galleries of West Chelsea, so there's plenty of civic history and trend-spotting to attend to before or after the concert.

THE INSIDE TRACK

jazz record CENTER

236 West 26th Street, Room 804

☎ 212 675 4480 | www.jazzrecordcenter.com

Ⓜ 23rd Street (C · E · F · V)

How many angels can dance on the head of a pin? As ontological puzzles go, that's the standard issue. But here's one that's just as difficult: How many LPs are stacked, floor to ceiling, in the Jazz Record Center?

"I can't answer that question," says Fred Cohen. Since he's the only person in the world who conceivably could, the query deserves to be supersized to the status of enigma. It's part of the allure of the store, one that Cohen, who buys and sells all those records, has been cultivating for 20 years. "I really have no idea," he insists. "This whole thing is a hobby that got out of hand. I haven't been miserable one day for it."

Cohen presides over a Borgesian library of vinyl arcana, the likes of which exists nowhere outside of public radio—probably. It's all jazz, from every era,

with some soul and gospel and blues thrown in for variety, plus CDs, DVDs, old magazines, posters, postcards, and other artifacts. The place seems to have everything that's jazz, short of actual instruments and the musicians to play them. "There's not enough room," Cohen concedes.

Though he's stumped by the volume of albums filling the loft-like, upstairs space, he knows what everything is worth. An obscure Tommy Flanagan disc briefly released (and then withdrawn) by a Swedish label in the mid-1950's fetched a whopping $2,000, for instance. But most collectibles are priced between $8 and $15. The most sought-after title? Miles Davis's 1959 materpiece *Kind of Blue*—which is also the best-selling jazz title in history. "It sells for upwards of $150, even for as much as $350," notes Cohen, who will give any record a test spin on one of two 1950's-era Thorens turntables he keeps running behind the counter. "It's one of the great prizes in any collection."

MIDTOWN

birdland

315 West 44th Street
between Eighth & Ninth Avenues
☎ 212 581 3080 | www.birdlandjazz.com
Ⓜ 42nd Street (A·C·E)

Not to be mistaken for the original Birdland, which was named for alto saxophonist Charlie "Yardbird" Parker and thrived on 52nd Street between 1949 and 1965, this Birdland is the latter-day version of what a stylish jazz club looks like. Tucked midway between Eighth and Ninth Avenues on 44th Street, the address is just far enough away from the theater district tourist crush to benefit from the foot traffic without being trapped by it. Though originally revived in 1986, in a smaller space on 106th Street, the franchise has been anchored here since 1995. The brassy décor, full restaurant, and dressy crowds mark it as a premium venue, as do its high-quality bookings,

Duke Ellington Orchestra (directed by Paul Mercer Ellington and Jack Jeffers)

and the expansive sweep of its main seating area, a dining room that faces the stage (access to the bar at stage left is cheaper, but there's less of a view). If the club was a suit it would be double-breasted. If it was a car, it would be a BMW (most jazz clubs are strictly Hyundai). Though, it's all relative. Compared to the cost of a Broadway theater ticket, dinner, drinks, and a show at Birdland looks like a bargain.

Birdland makes its reputation on its commitment to big bands and orchestral jazz, and the frequency with which its showcases first-rank players. Traditionally, Monday nights in Manhattan are the province of big bands—in part, because it's a slow night, and club owners figure it's something different; in part, because big bands always seem to play on Monday nights. Birdland expands on that premise. Chico O'Farrill's Afro-Cuban Jazz Big Band nails down Sundays, as it has for years, with the late trumpeter's arrangements and an all-star cast, led by his son, pianist Arturo O'Farrill. Mondays belong to Toshiko Akiyoshi's equally durable orchestra, featuring her husband, reeds-player Lew Tabackin. Tuesday is for Ellingtonia, with the current edition of the Duke Ellington ghost band, led by grandson Paul Mercer Ellington and Jack Jeffers. Other large ensembles find their way into the mix, as well as one-offs and extended runs by bandleader-composers such as Maria Schnieder, Andrew Hill, Lee Konitz, and Dave

Duke Ellington Orchestra

Duke Ellington Orchestra

Holland. Were Gil Evans, the orchestrator of such Miles Davis epics as *Sketches of Spain* and *Porgy and Bess*, alive and kicking, he'd probably have a weekly stint, too.

HISTORIC 52ND STREET

Compared to the much-diminished state of the jazz life in Manhattan today, the glory days of 52nd Street—aka Swing Street—must strike some ardent fans like a hallucination. The street blossomed between the end of Prohibition and the societal shifts that came after World War II. It was all of two blocks, running between Fifth and Seventh Avenues. But

the profusion of clubs that sprang up, drawing the greatest names in jazz, made it electric—the center of the universe for those who prized swing and, later, be-bop above all else.

The clubs, housed mostly in the unflattering brownstone basements of former speakeasies, sported evocative names: The Three Deuces, the Famous Door, the Spotlite, Jimmy Ryan's, the Onyx, the Yacht Club, Tondelayo's, Kelly's Stable, the Hickory House, the Carousel Club. William Gottlieb's famous

52nd Street, New York, ca. July 1948. Courtesy of William P. Gottlieb.

photograph captures the scene around 1948: a riot of neon and names flashing from marquee banners, the colors reflecting off of puddles in a damp street. It looks like the promise New York City made to the imaginations of small-town radio listeners of the day, leaning forward to hear a saxophone leap through the airwaves, and dreaming of the night.

As historian Scott DeVeaux notes in his study, *The Birth of BeBop*, a wartime cabaret tax encouraged the booking of small instrumental groups, whose performances were exempt. Scarcely any important jazz artist missed an opportunity to play 52nd Street, whether it was Billie Holiday, Fats Waller, Coleman Hawkins, Dizzy Gillespie, Roy Eldridge, Lennie Tristano, Stuff Smith, Hot Lips Page, Charlie Parker, or Miles Davis.

Not that Davis seemed to care for it much. As DeVeaux quotes him, the trumpeter shuddered at his first glimpse of the Three Deuces in 1944: "It had such a big reputation in the jazz scene that I thought it would be all plush and shit. The bandstand wasn't nothing but a little tiny space that could hardly hold a piano. ...I remember thinking that it wasn't nothing but a hole in the wall."

Compare that to jazz impresario George Wein's recollection. As a Boston high-schooler, he paid club-crazed visits to his older brother Larry, who was studying at New York University. The pair would roam from 7pm until daylight. Wein, thoroughly under age, would nurse a ginger ale at the bar to stretch his meager pocket change. "The highlight of the circuit was 52nd Street; it was one of heaven's avenues of gold," he writes in his autobiography. "...On a good night, you could walk into the Famous Door and see the whole Basie band crowded into the back of the room, swinging like mad."

Wein's avenue of gold wasn't paved so sweetly for very long. Gottlieb's photo seems to capture its high-flickering spirit just as its era was about to end. Strip clubs and such began to infiltrate, and the musical action was moving elsewhere. Even Charlie Parker had flown, a few blocks away, to lend his name to a new venue called Birdland. The bop era was in full fever, and Swing Street had swung its last.

café st. bart's

Park Avenue
at East 50th Street
☎ 212 888 2664 | www.jazzatnoon.com
Ⓜ Lexington Avenue (E·F·V) 51st Street (4·5·6)

This upscale restaurant hosts one of the more unusual jazz events in the city. Les Lieber's "Jazz at Noon" is a free weekly affair, staged Fridays at noon from mid-October through June. Lieber, who plays alto saxophone and penny whistle, and a dozen other enthusiasts from the corporate world bring their instruments, loosen their neckties, and ease into a relaxed jam session. Plenty of regulars drop by to swing a little, and remarkably so: The session's been going on for 38 years. But professional jazzers join in as well, as does each week's special guest. And the guests are no slouches. Their number has included alto saxophonist Ted Nash, guitarist Bucky Pizzarelli,

Diners at Jazz at Noon

reedsman Paquito D'Rivera, and trumpeter Claudio Roditi. In addition, jazz performances are sometimes staged on the outdoor terrace.

The setting is visibly historic: Nearby St. Bartholomew's Church, from which the cafe takes its name, is a mightily impressive Episcopal sanctuary which opened in 1918. Its stunning dome arrived in 1930, based on architect Bertram Grosvenor Goodhue's design for the dome of the California State Building at the 1911 San Diego Exposition.

CHEZ SUZETTE

675B Ninth Avenue
between West 46th & West 47th Streets
☎ 212 974 9002 | www.chezsuzettenyc.com
Ⓜ 42nd Street (A·C·E)

This much-admired French bistro has one of the
better reputations among old-line theater district
restaurants (it's been in business since 1967), and
a quaint niche in Hell's Kitchen—which is scarcely
hellish at all, anymore. Besides pâté and escargot, the
establishment also presents a different jazz vocalist
every night. The entertainment is free, and spans
a range from the Francophilic to standards to the
slightly further out.

cobi's place

158 West 48th Street
between Sixth & Seventh Avenues
☎ 516 922 2010
Ⓜ 50th Street (C·E)

Unique, especially among venues in the Midtown tourist district, Cobi's Place is, literally,
Cobi's—Cobi Narita, whose husband Sam Ash owns
the well-known music store downstairs from the
fourth floor space on West 48th Street. The 77-year-
old enthusiast, who has been active in the New York
jazz community for 40 years, founded Women in Jazz
in the late 1970's, and, a few years later, the Universal
Jazz Coalition/Jazz Center of New York. She also has
worked extensively with the jazz ministry of St. Peter's
Lutheran Church. It's quite a journey for Narita, who,
as a teenager during World War II was snatched away
with other Japanese-Americans to the Gila River
Detention Camp in Arizona.

Cobi's Place serves as an extension of Narita's
community mindedness. The focus is on all kinds
of jazz musicians—not only familiar names, but
complete unknowns with something to prove. Performances are not widely advertised, but are listed on
websites such as www.allaboutjazz.com. Reservations
are recommended.

iridium

1650 Broadway
at West 51st Street
☏ 212 582 2121 | www.iridiumjazzclub.com
Ⓜ 49th Street (N·R·W) 50th Street (1·9)

This blue-chip room is poised at a glittering junc-
ture. Just a few blocks north of Times Square, the
view from its street-level entrance is a snapshot any
tourist could love. Nearby, hoofers kick up their heels
on the Great White Way, while next door vacationing
Midwestern families join the singing waiters at one of
those faux-1950's diner-themed restaurants, belting
out their own lullaby of Broadway. Once upon a
time, the adjacent stretch of 52nd Street was a jazz
wonderland. Today, it's lucky enough that this Disney-
fied entertainment district can support the smattering
of jazz venues that it does.

Iridium fits the newly polished profile with
both flash and substance. It's one of the few music
establishments that means it when it claims to serve
food: pricey steaks and fancy Asian-themed appetiz-
ers, and a wine list you actually have to pause over.
And while its new location (the club opened in 1994
across the block from Lincoln Center, but moved in
2001) lacks the interior pizzazz of the Gaudi-meets-Dr.

Flora Purim and Airto: Airto Moreira

Seuss original, this simple, two-tiered, green-walled box of a space leaves little to focus on except the stage. What's comforting to know is that, even seated in a booth along the back wall, the sightlines are excellent—aided by professional lighting design that adjusts the mood accordingly. The sound system was hand-picked by Les Paul (see p. 98), the founding father of electric guitar, who has held court every Monday night since 1995. So you know that's taken care of. Musically, the club books a much wider range of players than you might expect anywhere north of Houston Street. Plenty of still-vital figures from a more golden jazz age—such as pianists Hank Jones, McCoy Tyner, and Andrew Hill, vibesman Bobby Hutcherson, and saxophonists Sam Rivers and Jackie McLean—check in for multi-night runs, something that keeps Iridium consistently on the map.

LES PAUL

Not much is constant in New York's jazz firmament. Favored clubs come and go. Great working bands get together, but can quickly disassemble as personalities or career motives dictate. The rule of thumb is: Enjoy it now, because tomorrow there will be something entirely different. The music stays fresh that way, but in jazz there's always a creative tension between tradition and innovation.

Then again, there's Les Paul. The guitarist reconciles the two seamlessly: He's the tradition *of* innovation. Right down to the nuts and bolts. Among many other items, Paul invented his solid-body electric guitar in 1941, using a 4x4 piece of pine with "wings" attached to it. It was dubbed "The Log," and could be amplified as loudly as necessary. (Unlike hollow body acoustic guitars, the instrument required a plug to be heard). Thus, rock'n'roll was made possible.

Paul relates his versions of this, and other bits of autobiography, every week at Iridium. Even though his official newsletter refers to him as "The Legend," Paul is an earthy soul who exists to blow raspberries at such notions. He's been playing somewhere in Manhattan every Monday night since 1984, though his first paying gig in the city was nearly 50 years earlier. The stint has become a ritual, beloved of tourists, ardent students of the guitar, and listeners who enjoy fleet, fancy picking complemented by the headliner's salty banter and quirky anecdotes. They line up outside the theater district site of Paul's current residency a full 30 minutes before showtime, in a queue that bends around the corner of Broadway and 51st Street. Some of the Paulites carry their own guitars (usually one of the Gibsons bearing the musician and designer's name), or an old LP. After the show, the same people will line up again for autographs. If an instrument or program isn't handy, Paul will genially take a Sharpie to an obeisant forehead.

Lester Polfus of Waukesha, Wisconsin, is 88 now. He wears a hearing aid, and spends as much time talking as playing the guitar (in league with guitarists Frank Vignola and Lou Pallo, and bassist Nicki Parrott). It's like Paul is fronting his own talk show, dishing up double-entendres, and reflecting on his

Les Paul at Iridium

days as an L.A. studio musician, telling tales on Bing
Crosby. When a guest musician sits in, and sometimes
very famous ones do, he finds every excuse to pick
on them—an affectionate hazing that turns the
subsequent performance into a dare and a gag. When
one visitor reeled off a particularly splendid take on
Django Reinhardt, Paul took a moment to illustrate
how he'd come up with that particular method first,
but then he delivers the punchline. He acts wounded:
"You had to wait until I was 88 years old before you
came over here to beat me up like that."

By the time the laughter subsides, the ensemble
has jumped into something old and familiar—"Brazil"
or "Sweet Georgia Brown" or "Tiger Rag"—and Paul
shows everyone why, despite creaky joints, his name
is literally synonymous with electric guitar.

For information, see Iridium (p. 96)

jazz standard

116 East 27th Street
between Park Avenue South & Lexington Avenue
☎ 212 576 2232 | www.jazzstandard.com
Ⓜ 28th Street (N·R·W·6)

O h, the conundrum of the jazz supper club! When music alone won't make a venue successful, the owner often decides to impose a menu and a drink minimum on patrons quite capable of burning their own mediocre cut of strip steak. And at a fraction of the price. Intrusive waitrons, ill-mannered diners smacking and slurping, the piercing jangle of cutlery—everything exists to distract you from the performers, who might as well return to the their long-forsaken Holiday Inn lounge gig. At least there, they got some respect.

That's a worst-case scenario, of course, though the experience is not uncommon to dedicated clubgoers and unfortunate tourists. But never at the Jazz Standard, where the concept of pairing live jazz with what used to be called "fine dining" actually works. Part of that is some fundamental respect for the separation of church and state, as it were. The Standard, a 250-person capacity club, occupies a plush and roomy basement space below Blue Smoke,

Ed Simon of the John Patitucci Group

an expansive barbecue restaurant and bar. Patrons who want to chow down can stick to the upper level. Jazz (and sometimes world music) fans can settle in downstairs, but still enjoy tangy chicken wings, pulled pork sandwiches, or mac-and-cheese from a smaller, club-sized menu. Or not. This charmed resolution to an age-old problem can be attributed to Danny Meyer. The prize-winning chef and longtime jazz-lover realized two dreams in 2001, when he took over the Standard (and its sister enterprise, the restaurant 27 Standard) from his first cousin, who had opened the Rose Hill club four years earlier. Meyer finally got the barbecue house he'd always wanted, and he'd be able to indulge his jazz fandom on a first-person basis. He's managed to bring a casual big city sensibility to both. Designer Peter Bentel gave upstairs (more dramatic) and downstairs (more romantic) a look that emphasizes physical comfort—cushy red booths high enough to vanish into—and industrial-tech style. "It's an urban joint," says Meyer, who wants to convey a certain downhome folksy flavor while avoiding a bait'n'tackle shop aesthetic. His advisors included documentarian Ken Burns (whose nearly 20 hours of *Jazz* put Louis Armstrong back on the charts again), who led Meyer to the photographer Charles Peterson, whose dozens of black-and-white images hang from the walls. The displays include many shots of jazz legends dressed to the nines for evenings of gourmandizing, babe-squeezing, and trading fours. Some of them are busy ripping through BBQ platters. One of pianist Thelonious Monk conveys a powerfully carnivorous mood: The brilliantly eccentric composer looks snazzy in his suit with the broad "Mr. B" lapels, staring with demonic focus at a pile of ribs gathered in his plate. Smoke curls upward from the cigarette between his fingertips.

"There's an inviting vibe about the place," says bassist and composer Ben Allison, part of a new generation of performers who have made the Standard a hub, often premiering new tunes, trying out new ensembles, or hosting week-long festivals. The venue frequently presents players from Allison's non-profit Jazz Composer's Alliance, and is a favorite spot for Palmetto Records, a top independent jazz label, to showcase artists' works-in-progress—as it did when renascent 1960's pianist Andrew Hill was prepping his big band for a recording session. "There's excellent sound. And the people who work there are very accommodating. The management is glad to see you. I'm not naming names, but jazz clubs are notorious for rude owners, and bad staffs that act too cool for the customers."

Since the Standard occupies a geographic middle ground between clubs uptown (conventionally, more geared to the tourist trade) and downtown (aggressively hip holes-in-the-wall), its bookings draw from the best of both worlds, which automatically makes the venue more progressive than most of its competition (which is to say, places with carpeting). It's distinguished, as well, by an earlier start time (the first set is at 7:30pm) and the abolition of the dreaded drink minimum, which usually runs $10. "I'd like to make jazz relevant to more people more of the time," says Meyer, a former jazz DJ in college who recalls welling up with tears immediately after reopening the Standard, when the South African pianist Abdullah Ibrahim headlined. "It feels like the jazz world can be too literate for its own good. I mean, why does everyone look at you like you're nuts when you say you're going to open up a jazz club?"

shelly's

104 West 57th Street
between Sixth & Seventh Avenues
☎ 212 245 2422 | www.shellysnewyork.com
Ⓜ 59th Street/Columbus Circle
(A·C·E·B·D·1·2·3·9) 57th Street (Q)

Once upon a time, this Deco-themed establishment was part of the post-Hard Rock Café/Planet Hollywood rush to tourist gold. But its tenure as the Motown Café was short-lived, and took a precipitous plunge into restaurant concept purgatory. New owners took possession three years ago and, behold, it was not the same old song. Shelly's, which serves up the

Nancy Kelly with Mark Taylor (drums), Neil Minor (bass), Dino Losito

kind of surf'n'turf cuisine Broadway show crowds consume most conspicuously, also more quietly hosts live jazz performances every night save Sunday up in its second floor Blue Lady Lounge.

While the walls vibrate with murals by ruckus-y types such as Red Grooms, and pop artists like Peter Max and LeRoy Neiman, the music calendar often is as lively. You can hear lusty, early-jazz specialists Warren Vache and Howard Alden, slinky crooners and torchlight divas, and off-duty Broadway singers, who entertain every Monday. Music typically begins at 7pm.

SWING 46

349 West 46th Street
between Eighth & Ninth Avenues
☎ 212 262 9554 | www.swing46.com
Ⓜ 42nd Street (A·C·E)

A mecca for dancers who want to relive the glory days of big band swing, this stylish supper club faces a quandary. In March 2003, the city's Department of Consumer Affairs ruled that the venue could no longer host dancers, claiming that it was in violation of zoning regulations. So, for now, at least, it's strictly listening—not ballroom. There's one exception: The Sunday "tap jam," which runs from 5 to 8pm and features such legends of the form as Dr. Jimmy Slyde.

It's open to all aspiring hoofers interested in developing their technique. The reprieve was won by Dr. Paul Chevigny, a law professor at New York University and the author of *Gigs: Jazz and the Cabaret Law in New York City*, who challenged the city's ruling. He defended the dance jam on grounds of freedom-of-expression.

Meanwhile, the club's calendar is packed with big band bookings and smaller combos, knowing revivalist crews that go by fanciful names: The Tiger Town Five, the Crescent City Maulers. Later evening sets often feature masters of the old school, such as trumpeter Warren Vache and guitarist Howard Alden.

Ron Sunshine and Full Swing

WOODY ALLEN

Cafe Carlyle

35 East 76th Street
between Madison & Park Avenues
☎ 212 570 7189
Ⓜ 77th Street (6)

Much as, say, a visit to the Statue of Liberty, or an afternoon munching hot dogs in the cheap seats at Yankee Stadium, there are specific sights and experiences that are quintessentially New York. The place would be a little less fun—and a lot less New York—without them. Look at Woody Allen. He's pulling a double shift, even. The guy who made *Manhattan*, and a score of other cinematic valentines to the city, has done more than any other filmmaker except Martin Scorsese to define his hometown on the big screen. Yet, as much as he loves New York, he also loves jazz. He loves old-time jazz, and he plays it every Monday night. He loves playing it so much he skipped the Oscars in 1978—the year *Annie Hall* swept the awards—because he didn't want to miss his weekly gig at Michael's Pub. These days, the engagement is at Cafe Carlyle, in the posh Upper East Side hotel, where Bobby Short frequently entertains. Mondays belong to Allen and a small group of musicians who play New Orleans-style jazz from the 1920's and 30's. There's not much fuss. Allen wanders in from a door at the end of the bar, settles at a table with his wife, Soon-Yi Previn, and their guests, opens up an instrument case and begins to assemble his clarinet. That's about as good as it gets for the celebrity gawk factor (unless, of course, that really is Peter Boyle sitting at their table, but the jury never reaches a verdict). Soon, the Woodman is on stage with his cohorts. He looks his age, 68, his nose offering a familiar perch for those signature glasses with their thick black frames. Eddy Davis, a banjo player whose endeavors include something called The New York Society for the Preservation of the Illegitimate Music, handles the arrangements. There's also a piano, drums, trumpet, trombone, and bass, with everyone—except Woody—pitching in on vocals. The music is the kind that Jelly Roll Morton and Louis Armstrong would have been conversant in, with selections like "Wild Man Blues" and "Dippermouth Blues," that are directly associated with them. The performances are jaunty and casually askew, making the most of the tunes' antique charms. Allen's no virtuoso, but he plays with focus and panache. The master of this form is a clarinet player named Ken Peplowski, who can sweep fluidly into the upper ranges and target tricky notes with a piercing attack. But the setting, which feels an awful lot like a scene in a Woody Allen film, doesn't call for such intensity. It's still spirited, which the music demands, but mellow enough not to rattle the mood of diners sipping on $20 cocktails. The intimacy of the room allows the music to breathe naturally, and if you're occupying one of the cheap seats ($40 scores a barstool), you'll be leaning forward once in a while to catch a stray lyric (or to crane your neck around one of the persistent shutterbugs who take photos throughout the hour-long show).

As New York rituals go, it's surprisingly cool. And Allen proves accommodating and gracious after he finishes off the night with a short trio set. A small crowd trails him out the exit door and into a hallway where he shyly dispenses autographs and receives the arms of strangers who pull him close, grinning for flashbulbs.

UPPER WEST SIDE

cleopatra's needle

2485 Broadway
between West 92nd & 93rd Streets
☎ 212 769 6969 | www.cleopatrasneedleny.com
Ⓜ 96th Street (1·9·2·3)

The real Cleopatra's Needle is an ancient obelisk that now resides on the Thames Embankment in London, where it's been since 1879—a long, long way from Heliopolis, where the Pharoah Thothmes III erected it around 1500 B.C. A second "needle" sits near East Drive at East 82nd Street, gifted by Egypt to New York City in 1881.

A neighborhood jazz hangout not far from Columbia University, this place—yet another Needle—can't claim such totemic antiquity. The moniker is simply a tip that its kitchen serves Middle Eastern fare. It's also one of the more musician-friendly rooms in town, particularly hospitable to students from the nearby Julliard and Manhattan Schools of Music, and jam session regulars who come by for the Monday night sessions overseen by pianist Eric Lewis.

MAKOR

35 West 67th Street
between Central Park West & Columbus Avenue
☎ 212 601 1000 | www.makor.org
Ⓜ 66th Street (1·9)

Truly a phenomenon of the Upper West Side: the non-profit cultural center as singles meet-and-greet. Founded by philanthropist Michael Steinhardt in 1999, Makor occupies a 5-story, 22,000-square

Cyro Baptista's Beat the Donkey

foot house that was built in 1904 and originally served as a residence for elderly Swiss women. In 2001, Steinhardt donated the $16 million property to the 92nd Street Y, which now operates its various facilities (which include a screening room, art gallery, gym, and classrooms). The downstairs performance space and bar draws scenesters in their 20's and 30's who know from Prada and don't mind a little high art with their cocktails. The emphasis is on Jewish cultural offerings—everything from klezmer to Kinky

(Friedman)—and the bookings are sharp enough to lure Rockport-shod downtowners onto the 1/9 line for a look-see.

They'll find it's worth the jaunt. The space, with its chic low-lighting and expansive bar, feels completely different from the building that houses it if not, in fact, like stepping into a parallel universe. The layout maximizes views of the stage, with the bar situated well behind the booths and tables in the main seating area. The venue aims for thoughtful, cross-cultural programming, but also attends to simply showing its constituency a real good time. Jazzier headliners have included Norah Jones, who enjoyed a pre-fame residency here, Kenny Garrett, Charlie Hunter, Bobby Watson, Marc Ribot, Anthony Coleman, James Carter, Leon Parker, Fred Hersch, Soulive, Christian McBride, Perry Robinson and the Jazz Mandolin Project. Not bad, especially within spitting distance of the Café des Artistes and Central Park. One caveat: Even though it's roomy enough for a couple hundred guests, the music room occasionally resounds with a lot of yada yada (moneyed singles plus mixed drinks, you do the math). In such cases, serious listeners are advised to scoot as close to the piano as possible.

SMOKE

2751 Broadway
between West 105th & West 106th Streets
☎ 212 864 6622 | www.smokejazz.com
Ⓜ 103rd Street (1·9)

Though it is something like the Holy Land to Sein-feldians, and stomping grounds for generations of Columbia students, the Upper West Side isn't the first stop that comes to mind on anyone's jazz itinerary. A few blocks up and over, there's Harlem, which boasts not only its resonant history but the kind of after-hours haunts that continue to bring that history to life. A short ride down Broadway brings you first to Jazz at Lincoln Center. Then, to a hub of "uptown" venues that faintly echo the vitality of a classic era amid the neon ruckus of the new Times Square. So there's no reason to expect any revelations in a part of town so thoroughly out-jazzed by its adjacent precincts.

Yet, that's what makes Smoke—which sits near the corner of Broadway and 105th Street—even more special. This venue's name evokes jazz iconography. Think of photographer Herman Leonard, whose black-and-white portraits of legends like Billie Holiday and Lester Young were typically cloaked in a halo of cigarette smoke. And it also reflects an aficionado's most approving verb: When the musicians *smoke* on the bandstand, it doesn't get any better. Ironic,

Eddie Henderson

then, that mayoral maneuvers have banned tobacco use in small bars such as this, which thrive on a kind of intimacy and atmosphere that evokes another time. But those qualities, at least, never go out of style, and Smoke rises to the occasion. Catching a late-night set here feels the way you always imagined a Gotham jazz hang should. That's especially true on weekends, when the bookings tap the frontlines of hard-bop veterans and adroit newbies, as well as name attractions who don't usually play clubs this small. Since the room only holds about 75 people, the Steinway grand piano sounds as clear from the far end of the vintage long bar as it does at one of the tightly clustered tables nestled at the lip of the stage. And since the decor suggests that of an agreeably distressed bordello—burgundy velvet drapes, faux tin ceiling, mahogany wood, aged brick walls and a hand-crafted banquette—it's easy to forget that you're in post-millennial Manhattan. When the alto saxophonist calls an old Charlie Parker tune, and bites into it fast with a flurry of fingertips and harmonic wizardry, the only time that really matters is the rhythm spilling out from the drumkit. But the truth is, even though Smoke is one of the city's newest jazz clubs—it opened in 1999—it's actually been around much longer. Before bartenders Paul Stache and Frank Christopher bought the place and refurbished it, the joint enjoyed a 22-year run as Augie's Jazz Bar. Its owner, who owns the unforgettable name of Augustus Quertas, ran it more like a social club than a business, cultivating the sort of loyal clientele whose collective affection for the barkeep's idiosyncrasies guaranteed him status as a local legend. Some of the keenest talents of a current generation of jazz artists, including pianists Brad Mehldau and Jackie Terrasson, started out at Augie's—and still visit Smoke, either to headline or to hang out. Another regular, back during his Columbia days, was the novelist and screenwriter Paul Auster, who paid his regards by immortalizing the still-quite-mortal Augie. Auster gave his name, and life story, to Harvey Keitel's rascal philsopher-cum-tobacco-vendor in—what else—*Smoke*.

JAZZ AT LINCOLN CENTER

alice Tully hall

1941 Broadway
at 65th Street
Ⓜ 66th Street (1·9)

frederick p. rose hall

Columbus Circle
☎ 212 258 9800 | www.jazzatlincolncenter.org
Ⓜ Columbus Circle (1·9)

While debates over the future of jazz will swirl as long as there's jazz to argue about, there's no question that Jazz at Lincoln Center has been a focal point in the discussion. The institution, which rose to prominence through the 1990's as a platform for trumpeter and Pulitzer Prize-winning composer Wynton Marsalis, is all about putting jazz in a historical context. Basically, that means giving it the same treatment other art forms—such as classical music—get at Lincoln Center. Jazz repertory, a movement that has grown stronger as the last of the music's legendary performers begin to fade from view, is in the foreground here, with concert programs devoted to the music of pantheon figures such as Duke Ellington, John Coltrane, and Thelonious Monk, and a tightly rehearsed big band to tour the world playing their music. J@LC, as it is billed, isn't alone among non-profit organizations promoting jazz concert seasons in New York, or revisiting the classics, or even fostering new works by contemporary jazz composers (which it does as well). But it is the largest and most influential, thanks to artistic director Marsalis's user-friendly charisma, strong funding from public and private sources, and an uptown pedigree that takes jazz out of the smoky barroom environments that spawned it and into tonier realms more often occupied by operas and orchestras.

Come the fall of 2004, J@LC will abandon its acoustically ill-suited base at Alice Tully Hall for what Marsalis calls the House of Swing: a dazzling new home on Columbus Circle. Dubbed Frederick P. Rose Hall—after the late real estate mogul who donated $10 million to the cause—the site will be contained within the 55-story, 2.77-million-square-foot Columbus Center, where AOL Time-Warner also will be headquartered. It could prove to be a Great Leap Forward, as J@LC will have to dramatically increase its programming—by 100 percent, in fact—to keep three separate performance spaces going. The primary theater, Rose Hall, will hold between 1,100 and 1,220 seats and emulate European opera house design, with an emphasis on an intimate feel even within a large space. A generous amount of vertical headroom—11 floors worth—makes triple-tiered seating possible, with only 80 feet separating the stage from the last, uppermost row. The Allen Room, a 300-600 seat space, will offer an entirely different perspective, as its amphitheatre-style seating will face a 50-foot glass wall with a view to Central Park. Beyond the skyline panorama, the room's other big attraction is its modular nature. Expect to see jazz and dance integrated here in a way that hasn't been possible for J@LC before, with events focused on, say, Brazilian themes, or swing dancing, that feature professional dancers as well as opportunities for the audience to get out on the floor. The third space will be named in honor of Dizzy Gillespie and a carbonated corporate sponsor: Dizzy's Club Coca-Cola. Designed as a 140-seat jazz club, the room will host live combos nightly with bookings separate from, but occasionally in parallel with, main stage performances. Another postcard view dominates the venue, which will offer lower admission prices than the other spaces (but still approximate to those of the city's blue-chip rooms).

Unlike its present accommodations on the Lincoln Center campus at 66th Street, the new site has the benefit of being designed with jazz specifically in mind.

The architect, Rafael Vinoly, sought to collapse the traditional distance between performers and audience, which is more appropriate to the communal spirit of jazz. The nature of the acoustics, which will be strongly influenced by Marsalis's input, will be warmer and less echo-prone than what classical halls offer—though the large theater space will also be used by classical orchestras. "We're going for the clearest sound," Marsalis has said, "but with warm and golden overtones: golden, but not too dark."

The challenge for the program will be to expand

its reach to match the potential of its new home, which also will include a rehearsal and recording studio, a broadcast center, a classroom and a jazz hall of fame named after the Eretegun family, which founded Atlantic Records.

"We're trying to become as inclusive and broad-based a jazz-presenting organization as possible without watering down the artistic integrity of what we present," says artistic administrator Todd Barkan, who promises that "the sky's the limit." What that means, among other things, is that J@LC will continue to move in directions it's already been heading: further explorations of Afro-Cuban and Brazilian traditions and overlaps, for instance, and jazz orchestra tributes to musical giants who missed out during the organization's first decade. The current season (2003-04) lauds both free-jazz innovator Ornette Coleman and beloved Kansas City pianist Mary Lou Williams. While Barkan does not see J@LC branching away from its foundation in swing-based jazz—an aesthetic the critic Albert Murray famously called "the velocity of celebration"—he does see programs conceived with "a little more imagination...You will see and hear all kinds of things."

TRiAd THEATRE

158 West 72nd Street
between Broadway & Columbus
☎ 212 362 2590
Ⓜ 72nd Street (1·9·2·3)

Two venues in one, the Triad consists of a small, street-level bar (the Dark Star Lounge) with a stage just big enough to welcome a drum kit for some combo action, and an upstairs "cabaret"-style theater with cocktail table seating on the floor and a steeply pitched balcony above. The staff is exceedingly friendly, and caters to the neighborhood's suit-and-tie crowd. The Triad hosts theatrical productions (such as *Boobs! The Musical*, tributes to Kurt Weill, and other half-a-block-off Broadway treats), and includes jazz in its musical mix. Aspiring vocalists, Cuban firebrands, free-jazz legends, they've all seasoned the room, which can comfortably hold about 130 patrons. The intimate setting and smooth acoustics only sweeten the pot. Call ahead or check listings for jazz events, as the theater is frequently booked with stage shows.

HARLEM

AMERiCAN LEGiON POST 398

248 West 132nd Street
between 7th & 8th Avenues
☎ 212 283 9701
Ⓜ 125th Street (A·C)

When people talk about Harlem's "down-home" flavor, they might have this joint in mind. The Sunday night jam sessions, now in their fifth consecutive year, summon a houseful of musical aspirants—and heavy hitters, as well. Hammond B-3 organist Seleno Clarke calls the shots. The onetime Basie sideman is the benevolent ruler here, leading off at 7pm each week with a bustling set of groove standards, eventually ceding the stage to the first of many jam enthusiasts. Sometimes, favorite sons such as drummer and singer Grady Tate stop by, just to raise the stakes. Admission is free (you simply have to sign the guestbook) and the kitchen will reward your patronage.

Lady Luci's COCKTAiL LOUNGE

2306 Frederick Douglass Boulevard
between 124th & 123rd Streets
☎ 646 548 0199
Ⓜ 125th Street (A·B·C·D·1·9)

For another angle on the Harlem jazz experience, and a great bargain as well, try this nightspot on Monday nights. That's when the Harlem Renaissance Orchestra holds sway, bustling with upwards of 16 members. The weekly brass explosion is the brainchild of Berta Indeed Productions, run by the same tireless jazz enthusiast who first instigated the Monday night jam sessions at St. Nick's Pub. The $10 admission (students, seniors, and the unemployed pay a little less) also includes gravy-sopping rights at the buffet table.

lenox lounqe

288 Lenox Avenue
at West 125th Street

☎ 212 427 0253 | www.lenoxlounge.com
Ⓜ 125th Street (2·3)

Harlem may be enjoying its second Renaissance.
Only a few years ago, those Striver's Row
brownstones were one of Manhattan's sweetest
real estate bargains. But prices have jumped. Now,
former president Bill Clinton keeps his office in the
neighborhood. Yet, it's still hard to find a cab after
dark. Such is prosperity. It's a different kind of heyday
than was first associated with these broad-shouldered
blocks—originally a Dutch settlement that was
exclusively white and fancy into the early part of the
20th century. The 1920's and 30's changed that image,
as Harlem became a platform for the emergence of
a new African-American consciousness in the arts.
This vibrancy was shared by jazz of the period: in the
eruptive improvising genius of Louis Armstrong, for
instance, and in the contagious zest of Duke Ellington's
Jungle Band, which reigned at the Cotton Club.

Earl May Quartet: Eddie Locke (drums) and Larry Ham (piano)

That era abides, if only in the sepia-toned reverie of Ken Burns documentaries and the jazz repertory movement championed by Wynton Marsalis and Jazz at Lincoln Center. It's history. Somehow, though, you can feel its authentic spark flickering at the Lenox Lounge. The club, which was built in 1939, is a gem: the last of the Art Deco bars in the city. Thanks to a $450,000 loan from the Upper Manhattan Empowerment Zone, the Lenox Lounge was restored in 2000, so that the way it looks now is as close as possible to the way it looked then. Glamor was social glue. Romare Bearden and James Baldwin once were in the house. So were Malcolm X and Langston Hughes. True, Billie Holiday no longer sits at her table—first one on the left—in the Zebra Room, which occupies the rear of the club, and is so named for its zebra-patterned wallpaper. There's a story behind the wallpaper, too: Seems the owners of a rival club, the El Morocco, didn't appreciate the lounge emulating its zebra theme, and initiated a dispute that kept the Lenox from opening until 1942.

Originally one of the Harlem clubs that presented black entertainers for exclusively white audiences, the lounge now draws all kinds of attention, much of it driven by a nostalgia for an era of uptown sophistication. The venue's vintage design is irresistible to contemporary celebrities and filmmakers. Everyone likes to use the club for a backdrop, whether in the

The Zebra Room at Lenox Lounge

Samuel L. Jackson remake of *Shaft* or for retro fashion shoots.

Despite the high style, the Lenox is very much a neighborhood bar. Live music here, which is not exclusively jazz, is the preserve of the Zebra Room, for which there is a cover charge. Often, there's a wholly different crowd listening in back than is drinking up front. The bar attracts a cross-section of patrons that is pure New York: plenty of Asian and European tourists, students over from nearby Columbia University, characters from around the block and dandies from the day, sage-like jazz aficionados who can tell you like it is—or was—and musicians chilling out before or after a set.

Roy Campbell Jr., is often among them. The trumpeter, one of the unsung heroes of the New York jazz scene, travels uptown and down all week long, gigging with all kinds of ensembles, working as a sideman and a leader, and exhaustively displaying the complete range of his horn. He has that encyclopedic mastery that comes only from playing every night, with peers at the top of their game. Mondays at the Lenox belong to Campbell, who leads a jam session and shows off the more mainstream side of his repertoire with a quartet. The engagement's lasted since 1996—a generation in the jazz life—and provides an excuse for players to come together informally. Sometimes they'll drop your jaw. Sometimes not, though Campbell promises that he doesn't chop heads (at least not here). "It's my community service project," he says. "It's not like at other places, where if you don't know a certain tune, then people start saying you ain't this or that. It's like a family thing, or church." Parishioners have included the rare Rock and Roll Hall of Famer (Lou Reed, who has a keen ear for jazz trumpeters, sat in one night), as well as players stepping out of the Jazz at Lincoln Center orbit, such as pianist Eric Reed, and the exceptional trombonist, Wycliffe Gordon. You never know, as Holiday once sang, what a little moonlight can do.

HISTORIC HARLEM

Harlem then and Harlem now means two vastly different things when it comes to jazz. Although the Apollo Theatre, which was refurbished and reopened in 1985 and now is owned by the state of New York, abides as a symbol of Harlem's past and present, it does so in a different context than in 1934, when its first amateur night lured hopefuls to the corner of 125th Street and Seventh Avenue. The 90-year-old structure, now managed as a non-profit and accorded historic landmark status, is a wonderful urban museum piece: the place for televised concert specials and awards ceremonies. Its revitalization speaks to the promise of an emerging Harlem of the 21st century, but it also stands as a nostalgic monument to the Harlem that was.

And yet, Harlem nostalgia is nothing new. More than 40 years ago, novelist and critic Ralph Ellison was already memorializing a time, a place, and a sound that was seminal to this neighborhood:

"It was itself a texture of fragments, repetitive, nervous, not fully formed; its melodic lines underground, secret and taunting; its riffs jeering—'Salt peanuts! Salt peanuts!'—its timbres flat or shrill, with a minimum of thrilling vibrato. Its rhythms were out of stride and seemingly arbitrary, its drummers frozen-faced introverts dedicated to chaos."

Ellison, writing in the January 1959 issue of *Esquire*, was describing "the rumpus at Minton's." As in Minton's Playhouse, a bar and music room that occupied the ground floor of the Cecil Hotel, at 210 West 118th Street. The rumpus was be-bop, or bop, "hardly more than a nonsense syllable," yet the term that would become most associated with the revolutionary sound birthed at Minton's in the early 1940's. Kenny Clarke, who redesigned the DNA of jazz drumming, was the linchpin of the house band. A then-unknown Thelonious Monk was the pianist. That's him, smiling broadly, in William Gottlieb's 1947 photograph, sharp in pinstripes, beret, and sunglasses, standing by the Minton's awning with some formidable company: trumpeters Howard McGhee and Roy Eldridge, and Teddy Hill, the tenor saxophonist and bandleader who

Arnett Cobb and Walter Buchanan, Apollo Theatre, New York, ca. Aug. 1947. Courtesy of the Gottlieb Collection.

managed the club. Dizzy Gillespie and Charlie Parker (upon arriving in New York in 1942) were mainstays, cooking up a brisk and bold new music in afterhours jam sessions. Charlie Christian, the legendary guitarist who brought the instrument out of the background and into the spotlight of jazz improvisation, found a home at Minton's and played there frequently. Lore has it that, though ailing from tuberculosis, Christian would rise from his sickbed, sneak over to the club, and play in the weeks before his untimely death, at age 25, in 1942.

Minton's provided an outlet, a safe harbor for musicians to visit on an off-night. Mondays the place was filled with band and cast members from the Apollo Theatre, who came for a free meal and stuck around to jam or to develop new tricks away from the particular rigors of the big band. "We invented our own way of getting from one place to the next," is how Gillespie described it in his memoir, *To Be or Not*

To Bop. And while Minton's was scarcely alone among significant Harlem nightspots—Monroe's Uptown House lays claim to a similar history—it occupies a mythic place in jazz lore. The site remains, now a residence for the elderly. Efforts by entrepreneurs, including Robert DeNiro, to reestablish Minton's have yet to be realized.

Equally as mythic was The Cotton Club—celebrated in Francis Ford Coppola's 1984 movie—which opened in 1923 at the Lenox Avenue site of the former Club Deluxe, which had been owned by Jack Johnson, the heavyweight boxing champ. The club, where top black entertainers played, sang, and danced for exclusively white audiences, was the brainchild of a mobster, Owney Madden. Back on the streets after an eight-year stint at Sing Sing, the convicted murderer needed an outlet to safely sell his beer despite Prohibition. The Cotton Club proved ideal, and not only for the bootleg business. The fancy showplace was pivotal in the career of Duke Ellington, whose orchestra held sway six nights a week between 1927 and 1931. Subsequent bandleaders included Cab Calloway and Jimmy Lunceford. The Cotton Club's reign was cut short in 1936 when racial discord made Harlem less secure for the venue's free-spending white patrons. The club closed, and reopened on West 48th Street, where it lasted another four years.

The 1930's Swing Era was epitomized by another fabled venue: The Savoy Ballroom. The massive dancehall sprawled across an entire block between 140th and 141st Streets along Lenox Avenue. Opening in 1926, the Savoy became the land of a thousand dances, a racially integrated club that fostered crazes such as the Lindy Hop and the Big Apple. The following January, drummer Chick Webb began performing with his orchestra there, and became a sensation. Webb, a hunchback whose growth was stunted by spinal tuberculosis, led his musicians from a centerstage platform where he sat behind a customized kit that included a 28-inch kick drum. He did not have the kind of star soloists that other big bands claimed, but he did make a major discovery: A 17-year-old orphan named Ella Fitzgerald. She joined the band in 1934, launching one of jazz's greatest careers. Webb achieved two pinnacles in 1937 and 1938, when he

Thelonius Monk, Howard McGhee, Roy Eldridge, and Teddy Hill, Minton's Playhouse, New York, ca. Sept. 1947. Courtesy of William P. Gottlieb.

trumped the groups of Benny Goodman and Count Basie in respective battles of the bands. His 1939 death left Fitzgerald in charge of the band, but the Swing Era had already begun its slow fade. Though the Savoy remained in business until 1958, it was, by then, the vestige of yet another phase in the history of jazz and of Harlem.

robin's nest restaurant & bar

457 West 125th Street
between Amsterdam & Morningside Avenues
☎ 212 316 6170
Ⓜ 125th Street (A · B · C · D · 1 · 9)

Home to a natural-born extrovert named Jimmy "Preacher" Robins, the Nest is true to its name: it's a cozy corner of the most mercantile and busily trafficked strip in today's Harlem—and a mere few minutes of highly aerobic stair-stepping through Morningside Park up to Amsterdam Avenue and the ivy airs of Columbia University. As befits the Southern-fried spirit of the venue, the Preacher commands a Hammond B-3 organ—once the very soul of every little bar in African-American neighborhoods nationwide, and an instrument that has become steadily more in vogue again as a new generation of jam bands rediscover the fundamental good times inherent in its warm, churchy grooves. The food served at the Nest matches the music in regionally grounded verve. The pig's feet and the greens can nourish the very souls "Preacher" Robins moves with his organ-playing and bluesy vocalizing. Live music, including rhythm-and-blues, prevails Thursdays through Saturdays, while Sundays finds the Preacher officiating over a gospel brunch.

st. nick's pub

773 St. Nicholas Avenue
near West 149th Street
☎ 212 283 9728
Ⓜ 145th Street (A)

No. 1 with a bullet among European tourists scoping out their authentic Harlem jazz experience, this downstairs bar a few blocks up from the 145th Street subway—where, yes, you can take the A train—is also good bet for those who don't have to sweat the exchange rate. The cover charge is only $3, and even that includes a piece of fried chicken with rice delivered to your table—if you ask nicely.

Mondays are devoted to late-night jam sessions, which are preceded by a couple of sets of more conventional combo jazz. The house band, fronted by saxophonist Patience Higgins, burns up the hard-bop canon, playing Sonny Rollins ("St. Thomas"), John Coltrane ("Mr. P.C."), and Kenny Dorham ("Blue Bossa"). Higgins draws on decades of touring and recording, including stints with rhythm-and-blues titans Wilson Pickett and Sam and Dave, and boasts an extroverted style customized for these occasions. Were this all, St. Nick's would still rate as one of the most enjoyable ways to kick-start the week, but the place exudes such personality that a visit quickly transcends the action on the bandstand. Higgins, a dapper gent who officiates before a wall poster of the lean, mean, young Miles Davis, may launch into a spontaneous diatribe against the evils of Kenny G. "It's not jazz, it's pop! Say it!" he beseeches, and the tightly packed crowd rallies in unison: "Pop!" Later, before playing an extended version of Marvin Gaye's "What's Goin' On?" he veers into politics, denouncing the Republican agenda with a humorously verbose fervor that prompts laughter and cheers. Is Bill Clinton in the house?

Audiences are conspicuously multilingual, as St. Nick's is a primary stop on many Harlem bus tours so popular with Europeans and Asians. But the neighborhood folks are just as present, whether knocking back a whiskey at the bar, carrying on an intense conversation with a table of first-time visitors, or squeezing their way across the floor to answer a pay phone that inexplicably rings on the wall near the bandstand. One regular, an older man dressed to the nines in a white suit and bowler hat, sits in the corner near the entrance, smiling quietly behind pitch-black shades. Before the night is done, Higgins will announce him as the winner of the "best-dressed man in Harlem" contest, and Mr. Gene Davis will be onstage, belting out a blues number. St. Nick's is famous for its jam sessions, which attract seasoned musicians (such as cornetist Olu Dara, who lives nearby) and sacrificial newbies game for a few competitive choruses. But, really, the show is always on. This bar used to be known as the Lucky Rendevous, and the sense of fortunate adventure that implies continues to hold true.

sHOWMANS

375 West 125th Street
between St. Nicholas & Morningside Avenues
☎ 212 864 8941
Ⓜ 125th Street (A · B · C · D)

Back when it first opened, in 1947, this nightspot was adjacent to the Apollo Theatre, whose entertainers considered the bar and restaurant their "living room." Showmans didn't become a music venue until 1978, and when it did, the sound was organized around a Hammond B-3 organ—the bedrock of groove-based black nightclub music, as epitomized by the likes of Jimmy Smith, Jack McDuff, and Charles Earland (and sampled on many a Beastie Boys 45).

Joey Morant

The club was forced to relocate, to Frederick Douglass Boulevard, after a 1985 fire, but owner Al Howard has persistently kept the faith. A 30-plus year veteran of the New York City Police Department, Howard was a supervisor of detectives chasing down the "Son of Sam" in 1977. But he nearly lost his bar in 1997, amid redevelopment plans for the Harlem USA urban mall. A new partner joined him, and Showmans reopened the next year at its current address.

The organ continues to reign supreme at Showmans, which features neighborhood jazz fixtures every night but Sunday, when it lures bigger names to its bandstand. The club does little to draw attention to itself, but creates an amiable environment for anyone who enjoys a home-style neighborhood jam—with a shot of whisky on the side.

sugar hill bistro

458 West 145th Street
between Convent & Amsterdam Avenues
☎ 212 491 5505 | www.sugarhillbistro.com
Ⓜ 145th Street (A·C·B·D·1·9)

Praise the Lord and pass the gravy. Much in keeping with the Southern tradition of massive pot-luck spreads served picnic style on church lawns after a long-winded morning service, the Harlem gospel brunch brings it all back home. This is true, even for secular humanists who have never dipped below the Mason-Dixon Line. Restaurants across Harlem open their doors on late Sunday mornings to accommodate thousands of hungry worshippers flooding out of services on the church-crowded blocks. Not all offer live music, but for those who like to stay in the spirit—or simply savor another aspect of Harlem culture—the gospel brunch can fill both the belly and the soul.

The weekly feed—a $22, all-you-can-eat deal—at the Sugar Hill Bistro cannot fail to sate. The atmosphere is casual but swanky: exposed brick and abstract paintings in a beautifully restored brownstone; diners seated family-style at long tables;

God's Grace performs at Gospel Brunch

fried chicken, grits, pancakes, sausage, pork-spiked greens, biscuits, and, yep, two kinds of gravy, abundant in steamy buffet serving trays. Near the entrance, in a small staging area, a big guy named AJ strives to work his audience into a fervor. But it's not quite happening. Everyone's obsessed with their vittles. The keyboardist, who accompanies the vocalist with jaunty syncopations and churchy chords, has already suggested the diners pick a designated driver. Once they go back for second helpings, a food-induced coma is likely imminent. But not if AJ can help it. He shakes his hips, winning some applause from the ladies, and works through a short set of R&B-flavored praise songs with gently positive themes. He's smooth and funky, without coming on too showily.

But that's only part of the show. The Bistro, one of the newer Harlem establishments offering this mix of food and entertainment, occupies a gem of a brownstone. Upstairs is a formal dining room, decorated with folk-art style portraits of jazz legends and gorgeously plush red velvet corner booths. There's live music, including jazz, during the week, and an art gallery.

Other notable brunch options:

copeland's

547 West 145th Street
between Broadway & Amsterdam
☎ 212 234 2357
Ⓜ 145th Street (1·9)

cotton club

656 West 125th Street
at Riverside Drive
☎ 212 663 7980 | www.cottonclub-newyork.com
Ⓜ 125th Street (1·9)

londel's supper club

2620 Frederick Douglass Boulevard
between 139th & 140th Streets
☎ 212 234 6114
Ⓜ 135th Street (B·C)

BROWNSTONES, BISCUITS & BEBOP

Harlem jazz strolls

☎ 718 680 6677 | www.SwingStreets.com

Harlem, in so many ways, evokes the ghosts of jazz past. The neighborhood is experiencing a welcome (from most vantage points) millennial shift, as business investments and a surge in real estate sales have begun to make the classic, far-uptown locale a newly desirable destination. So, perhaps, the promise of jazz future abides here as well. But, sadly, many of the historic jazz sites that put Harlem on the cultural map no longer exist. Hot spots such as the Savoy Ballroom and the original Cotton Club are long vanished. Vacant lots and bland urban shopping strips have taken their place, with a plaque stuck somewhere nearby to commemorate that which swung.

That's one of the more poignant aspects of Paul Blair's Sunday morning Harlem jazz walks. The Brooklyn-based journalist and historian actually leads three different tours of Harlem, as well as strolls through Midtown, Greenwich Village and the East Village, each glancing back at the comings and goings of jazz greats and great jazz venues. Blair's an affable sort who manages to reel off all sorts of minutiae without losing his audience. His original tour, titled "Brownstones, Biscuits and Bebop" covers central Harlem, with a casual amble over a nearly 20-block area beginning at 125th Street and Lenox Avenue and heading north, with particular attention paid to the streets between Lenox and 7th Avenue. Particularly fun is the walk down (West 133rd Street), a block that once was so thick with afterhours joints and basement clubs that it was called Jungle Alley. A litany of club names sounds like nothing so much as stray lyrics from an old blues song: The Nest, Basement Brownie's, Mother Shepherd's, Tillie's Chicken Shack, Pod and Jerry's Log Cabin, Mexico's. That was in the 1920's and '30's. The thing is, the street is still jumping. Only, at noontime on Sunday, the music pouring out of so many doors—even amplified through cheap speakers propped on porch steps—is gospel: fiery, footstomping, houserocking gospel. It's a resonant reminder of the dualities of Harlem musical life, and the rituals that define Saturday night and Sunday morning.

Blair also is good on the "Fats Waller slept here" details. You will learn, for instance, that Jelly Roll Morton lived at 209 W. 131st between Seventh and Fredrick Douglass avenues. That Langston Hughes spent two decades on the block of W. 127th Steet at Fifth Ave. That Roy Campanella sold liquor from a storefront at W. 134th Street and Seventh Ave., above the long-gone Clark Monroe's Uptown House—one of the seedbeds of bebop.

The tours come complete with an annotated homemade CD, which features relevant tracks: Cab Calloway vamping his way through a 1942 version of "I Get the Neck of the Chicken" or "Jumpin' at the Woodside," a 1938 tune, played by Count Basie's band (with Lester Young on tenor), and named after the hotel on Seventh Avenue near W. 142nd Street. By the time Blair concludes the walk, leading the way to one of the many neighborhood brunch spots, you'll be humming along with Cab and craving some soul food.

BROOKLYN & QUEENS

barbes

376 9th Street
at Sixth Avenue, Park Slope
☎ 718 965 9177 | www.barbesbrooklyn.com
Ⓜ Seventh Avenue (F)

Inspired by the North African cultural mix of their old neighborhood, a colorfully downmarket stretch in the 18th arrondissement of Paris, émigré musicians Olivier Conan and Vincent Douglas opened this small bar in rapidly upscaling Park Slope during the summer of 2001. The rundown site of a Chinese laundry for some 20 years and, briefly a campaign headquarters for failed mayoral candidate Mark Green, the storefront has been reborn as an homage to the African diaspora as it has infused French culture—among other tangents. Which means no Jerry Lewis tributes or—*quelle horreur!*—*Amelie*-themed drink specials; instead, the bar's performance space, a charming cafe-style anteroom, invites acts that offer endless variations on the uses of the accordion, bluegrass, and Balkan updates, and literary events (fitting, since one-man zeitgeist Dave Eggers launched McSweeney's while living a few doors down). Naturally, there's jazz, too: antique guitar tunes from the R. Crumb school of zoot-suit serenading, improvisatory summits featuring the latest wave of agents provocateur, the occasional 1960's legend, and crazy stomping brass ensembles. The bar's CD changer is loaded with classic jazz titles, so even at happy hour you can nurse your blues with Miles Davis.

bQE lOUNGE

300 North 6th Street
between Meeker & Havemeyer Streets, Williamsburg
☎ 718 388 2211 | www.bqelounge.com
Ⓜ Lorimer Street (L)

Close by the expressway it's named for, this Williamsburg nightspot has the clean, polished interior of something a bit more yuppie-fied than the warehouse block it sits on. Then again, that's the wave of the present in this madly popular neighborhood, whose influx of conspicuously under-30 scenesters has turned its once-industrial streets into an extension of the East Village's leisure zone. Jazz is far from a fixture here, but BQE is known to spotlight local acts on Mondays. There's comfortable seating, and some appealing nooks tucked away in the multi-leveled upstairs space.

GAlAPAGOS

70 North 6th Street
between Kent & Wythe Avenues, Williamsburg
☎ 718 384 4586 | www.galapagosartspace.com
Ⓜ Bedford Avenue (L)

An art-and-more bar and gallery located at the site of a former mayonnaise factory, Galapagos is the best-known of numerous new venues that began springing up in Williamsburg in the 1990's. The space is both a visual arts hub for the artist-dense neighborhood, a hangout, and a place to hear music in boho-friendly surroundings. Jazz is included, though often in a peripheral way. The Monday night burlesque revival shows share in some of the risque spirit of the early, bawdyhouse music with which Jelly Roll Morton made his name. Tuesday nights, which often boast a klezmer band, get a little closer to the mark. Up and coming neighborhood acts, such as the Gold Sparkle Trio, can also be counted on to make some trouble here.

HANK'S SALOON

46 Third Avenue
at Atlantic Avenue
☎ 718 625 8003 | www.hankstavern.com
Ⓜ Atlantic Avenue (2·3·4·5·Q) Pacific Street
(W·N·R·M)

About the last place anyone might mistake for a jazz hang, Hank's Saloon sits at the corner of an urban industrial strip—Brooklyn's Third Avenue—not far from the borough's downtown civic district. It is not a pretty sight, this ramshackle bar, with its mud-brown exterior enlivened by telltale flames, crudely flaring in yellow and red paint—suggestive of the label on a bottle of hot sauce or the tattoo bulging on a burly biker's Popeye-sized forearm. What tornado swept through rural Alabama and snatched this roadhouse into the skies, only to deposit it intact within spitting distance of the Long Island Railroad?

Don't ask. Just enjoy. The pub and poolroom hosts a late-night jam session every Wednesday that belies its rowdy-on-down reputation. The music's good, a reminder that even though most jazz musicians earn their living in Manhattan, a sizable number of them reside in near-Brooklyn—players like Ed Schuller, for instance, the bassist son of composer and conductor Gunther Schuller, who frequently shows up on Hank's bandstand.

pumpkins

1448 Nostrand Avenue
between Church Avenue & Martens Street
☎ 718 284 9086
Ⓜ Church Street (2)

Classic neighborhood club has been in business since 1978, which makes it the longest-running of the borough's current jazz venues. No pretensions here, and no cover charge, either. Vocalists, such as Miles Griffith (heard on Blood on the Fields), flock here with frequency, as do players taking a night off their regular gig and eager to jam. There's a two-drink minimum, a friendly reputation, and live music every night.

sista's place

456 Nostrand Avenue
off Jefferson Avenue, Bedford-Stuyvesant
☎ 718 398 1766
Ⓜ Bedford Avenue/Nostrand Avenue (G)

The Bedford-Stuyvesant coffeehouse and community center, with roots deep in social activist movements, offers everything from poetry workshops to political forums. Jazz is a cental factor, as well, with Saturday evening performances curated by former Sun Ra trumpeter Ahmed Abdullah. The music is first-rate, with such performers as guitarist and singer Olu Dara, drummer Lewis Nash and bassist William Parker leading their outfits. Admission is sensible (about $10), and tea or coffee is served instead of alcohol. Call ahead for information and listings, as jazz is not programmed year-round.

HOME WITH SATCHMO

louis armstrong
house & archives

Queens College, 65-30 Kissena Boulevard, Flushing

☎ 718 997 3670 | www.satchmo.net

Ⓜ 103rd Street/Corona Plaza (7)

Monday–Friday, 10am–5pm or by appointment

To the Library at Queens College:

Ⓜ Seventy-First Avenue & Continental Ave (E·F)

Bus: Q65 to Jewel Avenue & 150th Street

Queens' most-celebrated jazz resident is quite a bit more than a memory. Besides conceiving the template for jazz trumpet, instigating the concept of solo improvisation, and becoming a pop vocal artist widely loved beyond the jazz realm, Louis Armstrong was a loyal neighborhood guy. He was deeply invested in the daily life around his modest brick home in Corona, where he moved in 1943. He also was a pack rat, errr—relentless collector of his own ephemera, that is—and so, more than 30 years after his death in 1971, there exists an abundance of Armstrong effects and memorabilia. It's in the collection of the Louis Armstrong House & Archives at Queens College, to which a visit is more uniquely rewarding than many such places. Much of that has to do with Armstrong himself, a character of marvelous self-invention who could easily have sprung from the depths of American folklore if, in fact, he had not already risen from the hazard-strewn streets of New Orleans. Even the date given as his birthday—July 4, 1900—has a mythic ring to it: Born with the century, on Independence Day. Well, who else so fully exemplified jazz? The singularly American art form began as the creative expression of musicians only a generation removed from slavery. It doesn't really matter that Armstrong—who was also called Pops, or Dippermouth or Satchelmouth or Satchmo—was actually born a little more than a year later. Like so much in his life, it just makes for a better story. That Armstrong preserved so much of that story while still alive and blowing strongly has guaranteed a healthy afterlife that isn't limited to his recorded musical legacy—or the many movie cameos he made during his glory days.

Efforts to complete a $1.6 million restoration of the home he shared with his fourth wife, Lucille, should now be realized, and the house, at 34-56 107th Street is slated to be officially open to the public in Fall 2003. The actual archives are housed in a library space at Queens College, which has been overseen by archivist Michael Cogswell since 1991. The collection includes more than 5,000 items. These number a remarkable trove of 650 reel-to-reel audio tapes made by Armstrong, recorded between the early 1950's and the week before his death. (The tapes are gradually being converted to CD format so visitors can listen to the recordings). An enthusiastic consumer of hi-fi electronics, the trumpeter would likely be agog at the digital advancements of iPods, MP3 downloading, and rip-and-burn CDs—and the first on his block to make use of them. But he also displays a visual flair, as each box of tape is decorated with an original collage, often made from cut-up newspaper and magazine clippings about Armstrong or his contemporaries. In one, an image of King Oliver—Armstrong's trumpet-playing forebear—hoists his horn from an imaginary stage inside a clipping of the artist's head.

It's those sorts of details you have to love. Poster-size blowups of Armstrong's letters are, as might be expected, laden with frisky humor. There are samples of risque poetry; a holiday card with a photo of him sitting on a toilet (as viewed through a keyhole)—the musician was a great advocate of the laxative Swiss Kriss, and gave it away to friends and fans; and a Cannabis Cup awarded posthumously by *High Times* magazine (Armstrong was also a big fan of marijuana, and titled an unpublished volume of his autobiography "Gage," which was a slang term for the weed). The Archives curates accordingly, with an affectionate wink. One of its recent exhibits: "Love Me or Leave Me: Louis and His Four Wives."

up over jazz cafe

351 Flatbush Avenue
at Sterling Place
☎ 718 398 5413 | www.upoverjazz.com
Ⓜ Seventh Avenue (Q) Grand Army Plaza (2·3)

Regulars swear by the Monday night jam sessions at this neighborhood spot, dubbed the "Up Over" due to its second-story perch above Flatbush Avenue—where it sits adjacent to Park Slope, Prospect Heights, the Brooklyn Museum of Art, and the downtown Metro Tech area. Top-flight alto saxophonist Vincent Herring is frequently in residence, and big names have been known to surprise audiences with late-night appearances. The club tends to book names familiar to long-time listeners, such as Grady Tate—an immaculate drummer who also loves to vocalize—saxophonist James Spaulding, and former Sun Ra trumpeter Ahmed Abdullah. A modest door fee of $10 prevails most evenings, with a drink minimum.

Anthony Wonsey

QUEENS JAZZ TRAIL

flushing town hall

137-35 Northern Boulevard, Flushing
☎ 718 463 7700 | www.flushingtownhall.org
Ⓜ Main Street (7)
Exit and walk north on Main Street to Northern
Boulevard. Turn right and walk about two blocks
to 137-35 Northern Boulevard.

Though Manhattan had most of the nightlife, the
sprawling borough of Queens was—historically—
where many of jazz's great names actually went home
to sleep. The fact is not lost on the Flushing Council
on Culture, and Flushing Town Hall, which does its
best to promote the local jazz legacy through exhibits,
concert performances, and a popular Saturday
morning bus and walking tour. The Queens Jazz Trail
Tour is a three-hour jaunt in an old-fashioned trolley
style bus through the jazziest parts of Queens. Louis
Armstrong's Corona is a primary stop, including peeks
inside Joe's Artistic Barber Shop—where Satchmo had
his hair cut—and the house where Armstrong lived,
which has been renovated for a fall 2003 reopening.
Tour guide Coby Knight—a cordial amateur vocalist
and doo-wop warrior who grew up in Corona with
fond memories of its African-Amercian musicians and
sports champs—is quick to remind everyone that it's
not all about Louis. Dizzy Gillespie also lived in the
neighborhood, as do Clark Terry and Jimmy Heath
today. Other residents of Queens, at large, included
Charles Mingus, Roy Eldridge, Buddy Rich, Lennie
Tristano, Milt Jackson, Benny Goodman, John Coltrane,
Mal Waldron, Lester Young, and Bix Beiderbecke.

A visit to the Armstrong archives at Queens
College (see p. 147) sketches in much about the
trumpeter's homelife, one frequently devoted to
entertaining grinning posses of kids from the block.
And a further jog into St. Albans, and a walking tour
of Addisleigh Park, explores a neighborhood where
the top black entertainers of their day enjoyed a kind
of exclusive community. Count Basie, Ella Fitzgerald,
Fats Waller, James Brown, and Lena Horne all called
its verdant lawns home. The trend began in the
1920's, as segregation deterred the performers from

buying homes elsewhere. Until his death, the bassist Milt Hinton would welcome tour groups into his house for a brief look-see and some refreshments. And even though Count Basie's Olympic-sized swimming pool is a thing of the past, his old spread now subdivided, there's still a chance to bump into a few active characters: Hornmen Illinois Jacquet and his brother Russell still live in the park, right next door to each other.

BEYOND THE CLUBS

JAZZ FESTIVALS

jvc jazz festival

Various sites each June
www.festivalproductions.net

verizon music festival

Dates and sites TBA
www.festivalproductions.net

Jerry Stiller, playing George Costanza's holiday-crazed father on *Seinfeld*, had a word for it: Festivus. Translation: The season when everyone celebrates with huge meals and endless gatherings. Jazz fans in New York have their own Festivus, which begins in late May, sprawls across the entire month of June, and spills over into July. Different years bring different sponsors, organizers, and themes, but the most consistent—if not always the most creative—of the summer's big events is the JVC Jazz Festival. Masterminded by George Wein, the promoter behind the fabled Newport Jazz and Folk Festivals of the 1950's and 60's, and the massive New Orleans Jazz & Heritage Festival, the citywide June jazz summit has been a staple of Manhattan life since 1972. Wein was forced to move his event from the open-air setting of Newport, Rhode Island (a smaller festival has since been reactivated) after unruly crowds scared off the city fathers. The inaugural season was auspicious. A July 4 concert paired the Charles Mingus orchestra and Ornette Coleman—performing *Skies of America* with the American Symphony Orchestra—on a double-bill at Philharmonic Hall.

That was 31 years ago. As the roster of jazz giants has dwindled, Wein's festival has struggled for relevance. He's also traded fire with critics who were perhaps too eager to send the now-78-year-old entrepreneur out to pasture. Not so fast. Throughout the 1990's, the Knitting Factory's upstart "What Is Jazz?" fest grew bigger each year as sponsors (Heineken, Texaco, Bell Atlantic) came and went. By 2000, it had become the dominant New York jazz festival, splitting June evenly with Wein (JVC runs for two weeks, beginning in mid-June), and incorporating major mainstream names into its mix of downtown favorites and rock acts (such as Sonic Youth and Stereolab). Blink. Within a year, Wein's outfit—Festival Productions—snatched the financially shaky Knitting Factory's main sponsor, Verizon, and put on a second, smaller late-summer festival, Verizon Music Festival, that featured concerts identical to what the venue then typically programmed. Dominance ensured, Wein has subsequently become a touch more inventive with his primary summer smorgasbord. The 2003 fest, while still broadly tribute-oriented (Bix Lives!), continued a welcome expansion from major concert halls and parks into small clubs such as the Village Vanguard, and tapped into a new generation of players to complement the blue-chip bookings of Ornette Coleman, Wayne Shorter, Keith Jarrett, and other major artists who first made their names in the 1960's. "The jazz press has often seized upon emergent activity as an excuse to cast our festival in an adversarial role," the not-unprickly Wein writes in his memoir, *Myself Among Others: A Life in Music* (Da Capo). "...This epidemic started as far back as the late 50's." Unfazed, the promoter sticks to his program, and still finds time to jump onstage and play a little piano.

vision festival

Held during late May
Site TBA
www.visionfestival.org

Stridently modest, the Vision Festival—an artist-run event with roots in the Lower East Side jazz collectives of the 1980's—arrives each May as a teaser for Festival Month. Its length varies between one week and two. Each year's performance site is similarly unpredictable. But artistic director Patricia Nicholson Parker has displayed an uncanny knack for securing offbeat, and often historically significant, venues to host the shebang. During its eight-year run, the non-profit festival has been housed in a dilapidated former synagogue, the basement of a Greek Orthodox church, a rehab center that had once been the site of 1960's rock palace the Electric Circus, and the Knitting Factory, whose own corporate-backed summer festival it ostensibly rivaled. Of late, Vision unfolds in trendy NoLiTa, in a spacious recreation hall owned by St. Patrick's "Old" Cathedral—first built in 1815, and restored after an 1868 fire, it's the city's oldest Catholic cathedral. The Mulberry Street site provides a suitably informal backdrop for the fest, which mingles generations of forward-minded musicians, dancers, poets, and visual artists in marathon evenings of nervy new sounds—and flashbacks to the days when jazz was animated by an activist spirit.

jazz in july festival

1395 Lexington Avenue 92nd Street

☎ 212 875 5766 | www.92Y.org

Pianist and historian Dick Hyman's annual celebration of vintage jazz, staged at the 92nd Street Y. Jazz finds its way into various other summer festivals, special occasions or ongoing outdoor performance seasons. Check out these for starters.

hudson river festival

Summer-long in Battery Park City
www.hudsonriverfestival.com

lincoln center out of doors

Various sites at Lincoln Center
Throughout August
www.lincolncenter.org

JAZZ RADIO

When it comes to jazz broadcasting in New York, Bird is the word. Every weekday morning, longtime radio host Phil Schaap plays the music of Charlie Parker on **WKCR-FM** (89.9), the non-commercial station based at Columbia University. Schaap, affectionately known as the "Bird Nerd," hits the air at 8:20am, and keeps it filled with sometimes rare recordings and lots of aficionado banter. It's the stuff of classic radio—evoking not only the bop yesteryear, but the era when radio was still the dominant form of electronic media and New York was in post-war creative ferment.

WKCR's signal first crackled about the time Parker and his cohorts were revolutionizing jazz: 1941. Initiated as a student radio club with transmissions limited to dorm rooms, the station went public on October 10. The first record to spin was "Swing Is Here," featuring Gene Krupa and Roy Eldridge. Jack Kerouac, then a Columbia student, would have had his ear glued to the dial. And, as Schaap notes in an extensive interview on the station's website (www.wkcr.org), Bela Bartok—who taught music at Columbia and who was an occasional guest—was petitioned for his thoughts on Coleman Hawkins' "Body and Soul."

Six decades on, WKCR continues to program copious (but not exclusively so) amounts of jazz, with 30-year veteran Schaap and his fellow hosts on hand to ensure an in-depth historical focus that is also obsessively anecdotal. The station is famous for its marathon celebrations of a particular artist—playing nothing but Thelonious Monk or Eric Dolphy on their birthdays, or perhaps the anniversary of their deaths—which can stretch to as long as 12 days. During one such festival, in July 1979, honoree Miles Davis phoned WKCR a lot. During one such conversation, which lasted two hours, Schaap recalls jotting down a long list of Japanese-only Davis discographic information as the temperamental trumpeter dictated. "He said, 'You got it?' I said, 'Yes, Mr. Davis.'—I Mr. Davis-ed him the whole week, to be truthful. And he said, 'Good. Now forget it. Forget it. And play *Sketches of Spain* right now!' So I walked into master control, and just to make it more dramatic, I picked up the needle with the pot [volume knob] up, and plunked it down hot."

Some other jazz radio options:

WBGO-FM (88.3): Newark-based public radio station programs jazz 24/7. Along with shows overseen by longtime hosts such as Michael Bourne ("Singers Unlimited," Sundays at 10am) and Walter Wade ("Fillet of Soul," Sundays at 6:30pm), the station carries the full range of NPR syndicated jazz programs. www.wbgo.org

WFMU-FM (91.1): As its motto states, this Jersey City, N.J.-based community radio station has been "freeing your ass so your mind can follow since 1958." Jazz occasionally intrudes on the madly eclectic shows—which go by names like "Inflatable Squirrel Carcass"—programmed by a diverse and quirky array of volunteer DJs. Bethany Ryker's Sunday night "Stochastio Hit Parade" (10pm-midnight) is often a treat, with live interviews and performances from downtown faves, and no lack of conceptual bravado ("Brass Meets Bollywood" is a typical theme). www.wfmu.org

WNYC-FM (93.9): Cultural institution Jonathan Schwartz spins American popular song, including the great jazz vocalists, Saturdays and Sundays at noon. Also: "Big Band Sounds" with Danny Stiles, the "Vicar of Vintage," 8pm Saturdays on the station's other outlet, AM 820. www.wnyu.org

OTHER VENUES

Many museums, universities and non-profit arts organizations present jazz throughout the year, or on specific occasions. Here's a shortlist of institutions that offer interesting and consistent programming.

Tribeca Performing Arts Center

Borough of Manhattan Community College
199 Chambers Street, #S110B
near West Side Highway
☎ 212 220 1460 | www.tribecapac.org
Ⓜ Chambers Street (1·2·3·9)

Home to the Lost Jazz Shrines performance series, an ongoing historical glance at jazz venues that no longer exist—yet contributed something invaluable to the evolution of the form. Each May and June, a selection of concerts focuses on artists and styles associated with particular jazz eras and clubs. Previous tributes have been paid to the Half Note, Slug's, the Five Spot, Café Society, and the Loft Scene of the 1970's. The center, which has a roomy, modern-tech style auditorium, also presents a variety of other entertainments, including other jazz performances and programs during the annual Tribeca Film Festival.

The New School

55 West 13th Street, 5th Floor
between Fifth & Sixth Avenues
☎ 212 229 5896 x305 | www.newschool.edu/jazz
Ⓜ 14th Street (A·C·E·F·L·1·9·2·3)

The jazz program at the downtown university, located near New York University and the West Village, has quite a reputation in town. Its faculty includes such players as Cecil Bridgewater, Jane Ira Bloom, Andrew Cyrille, Joe Chambers, Chico Hamilton, Junior Mance, Benny Powell, Reggie Workman, and many others. And its roster of graduates boasts some of the most promising younger jazz musicians in the field: Brad Mehldau, Chris Potter, Roy Hargrove, Peter Bernstein, Miri Ben-Ari, Susie Ibarra, Jesse Davis, and Walter

Blanding Jr. Live performance is a constant here, from faculty concerts to special collaborative events featuring guest artist-educators in league with their students, as well as solo and ensemble recitals. Times vary, but there's frequently something going on in the Jazz Performance Space, a fifth floor venue where admission is always free and open to the public.

ROSE CENTER for EARTH ANd SPACE AT THE AMERICAN MUSEUM of NATURAL HISTORY

81st Street
at Central Park West
☎ 212 769 5200 | www.amnh.org
Ⓜ 81st Street (B·D·C)

Live jazz, under the Sphere at what is also known as the Hayden Planetarium, is presented the first Friday of each month, with sets at 5:45 and 7:15pm. Free with regular museum admission. Bookings have included well-regarded jazz veterans, such as Jimmy Heath, Lou Donaldson, and David "Fathead" Newman.

SYMPHONY SPACE

2537 Broadway
at 95th Street.
☎ 212 864 5400 | www.symphonyspace.org
Ⓜ 96th Street (1·2·3)

Imaginative jazz programs are a highly visible component of this uptown non-profit venue's extensive calendar of performances, readings, and screenings. Home to the World Music Institute, as well as two separate theaters (including the Leonard Nimoy Thalia, named after its "Star Trek" star patron), Symphony Space is best known to jazz fans for its annual "Wall-to-Wall" concerts. The free, day-long events unite a seemingly irrational array of artists around the music of a single composer. Miles Davis and Joni Mitchell have been previous subjects, while the names on the musician's call sheet would reflect smartly in anyone's record collection. There are evenings built around individual leaders (such as Don Byron, Jason Moran) and their concepts, and quasi-jazz occasions that are compelling for their trans-genre overlap, such as the Bang-On-a-Can Marathon (contemporary classical music a-go-go) and guitarist Gary Lucas' Captain Beefheart Project.

miller theatre

Broadway at 116th Street
☏ 212 854 7799 | www.millertheatre.com
Ⓜ 116th Street (1.9)

Columbia University's performing arts center has devoted itself to presenting music by contemporary composers from all over the map—from upstarts like the Bang on a Can All-Stars to high priests such as Elliot Carter—with crossovers between genres encouraged. There's room for jazz within the chamber-music agenda. Eric Reed, a pianist who has logged many tours and sessions with the Lincoln Center Jazz Orchestra and Wynton Marsalis, curates a jazz concert series each year with an eye toward mainstream player-composers and underappreciated, yet strongly influential artists such as pianist Donald Brown and Ellington composer Billy Strayhorn.

bamcafe

30 Lafayette Avenue
between Lafayette & Ashland Streets, Fort Greene
☏ 718 636 4100 | www.bam.org
Ⓜ Atlantic Avenue (2·3·4·5·Q)
Pacific Street (W·M·N·R) Fulton Street (G)
Lafayette Avenue (C)

Smartly curated, this ancillary performance space at the Brooklyn Academy of Music offers hip weekend shows that frequently tap the upper echelon of jazz thinkers—or, at least, tweak the norm in fun and thoughtful ways. Admission is free, with a $10 drink and food minimum, but it's a good idea to call ahead for reservations.

laGuardia performing Arts Center

47th Avenue & Van Dam Street
Long Island City, Queens
☎ 718 482 5151 | www.lagcc.cuny.edu/lpac/
Ⓜ 33rd Street (7)

Venue at LaGuardia Community College in Queens features jazz in its mix, presenting a variety of programs, including celebrations of Queens' jazz heritage, Latin-themed concerts, and evenings focused around specific musicians.

INDEX

alphabetical index

Neighborhood Index

sidebars

ABOUT THE AUTHOR

Steve Dollar writes about pop culture for a variety of publications, including *Newsday*, *Playboy.com* and the *Atlanta Journal-Constitution*, where he was the chief pop music critic for the better part of the 1990's. He also has contributed to the *Wall Street Journal*, *GQ*, the *Oxford American*, and the *Rolling Stone Encyclopedia of Rock & Roll*. He lives in New York City.

ABOUT THE PHOTOGRAPHER

Nicholas Prior's images have been published and exhibited across the country. He holds a Master of Fine Arts degree in photography and related media from the School of Visual Arts in New York City. For more information about his work please visit NicholasPrior.com.

NOTES

NOTES

NOTES

NOTES